PRAISE FOR
EMMELIE PROPHÈTE

"During a stopover in Miami, a young Haitian traveler scrolls through the lives of three women—those of her mother and her sisters—made up of servitude (under the weight of lying men), of exile (where love is a bad necessity), and of forgetting (in a world that can exist without them). They stood up; she can testify. *Blue (Le testament des solitudes)* is the fierce heritage of any (Black) woman."

—Johary Ravaloson, author of *Return to the Enchanted Island*

BLUE

BLUE

TRANSLATED BY TINA KOVER

EMMELIE PROPHÈTE

Text copyright © 2013 by Emmelie Prophète
Translation copyright © 2022 by Tina Kover
All rights reserved.

Previously published as *Le testament des solitudes* by Éditions Mémoire d'encrier in Canada. Translated from French by Tina Kover. First published in English by Amazon Crossing in 2022.

Published by Amazon Crossing, Seattle

www.apub.com

Amazon, the Amazon logo, and Amazon Crossing are trademarks of Amazon.com, Inc., or its affiliates.

ISBN-13: 9781542031318 (hardcover)
ISBN-10: 1542031311 (hardcover)

ISBN-13: 9781542031295 (paperback)
ISBN-10: 154203129X (paperback)

Cover design by Faceout Studio, Tim Green

Cover image © Tamara Natalie Madden / Bridgeman Images

Printed in the United States of America

First edition

BLUE

I

The land seems boundless here. Life curled in, folded onto itself. Seen from here, the world is immense and small at the same time. All this green. These wetlands are, and have always been, imaginary fences.

The war was over, people said. The girls had heard nothing, understood nothing about that war. *Nazis* and *Allies* meant nothing to them. The world hardly communicated at all with the *province bleue*, buried deep in a country mired forever in the Caribbean Sea, in misery. It was a world far from the world, a world you had to leave in order to live.

Three girls, born here when it was no place to be born and no place to be female. Between dead fields and bleak rivers, the only dream they had inherited was the dream of leaving. Going far away from this silent stepmother of a land. The road that led to school was too long. They didn't see why it was necessary to go there so early every morning, half asleep, bellies empty, to come home too late, too tired to face the household chores expected of girls.

It's a story I've heard dozens of times, one I never really thought I was giving much attention, even as it settled into my mind, heavy and soft, as only a mother's legacy can be.

My mother, her two sisters, eyes glued to that endless road that led to the city, the city of a thousand faces, a thousand chances, a thousand tomorrows. *Would the coffee taste different?* they wondered after the lamp was turned off. Eyes open, they listened to the insects that seemed to fill the night in their thousands, complicit in their desires, their plans to go.

The story is hazy, unknown, or nearly so. Snippets of uncertainty, time consigned to illegible notebooks. There should be no memory of it, no testament.

Three women ready to leave, to plunge into the violence of the city, into the scent of men. Happiness always a bit further away, their backs turned to the passage of time. Three lost souls, certain it was mere bad luck that had caused them to be born in this remote place. Sisters in memory, in desire, in destiny.

My mother has no real identity to speak of. Odile and Christie, maybe. By the end of the story, or what will seem to be the end, they will seem like nothing but an endless cry echoing from the depths of this country. A cry that stretches from here to the Atlantic every day, that lies in wait for us and disrupts our lives. Public gardens cut through by wind and shadows, offered up as fodder for broken dreams.

They left. One after another. And now, a whole America later, I have received pages of solitude, words locked twice, battles to fight again.

II

Journeys always ended with a coffee. I loved the taste of airports.

For a week I had hauled thousands of images of them around with me. Unfinished business had caught up with me again. Faces—related, loved, lost in unknown lands—departed without the usual words of affection, without keeping up appearances. Love, for these women, has always been a necessary evil, a miserable transaction.

I'll never know anything but the end of these stories: a casket lowered into a hole amid a commotion of flowers and grief. Sandy paths, moons to see by, to grow by, to be frightened by, to cheat solitude by.

The words had rarely given me a choice; they crept in late at night, like dauntless explorers of time. I am always too eager to get away with my images. My sleeves hang, overlong, in the crowd. I will always love taking journeys. The ones I've taken alone in my head and in the cold. The ones I'm still trying to take. A path of flesh. A city of madness.

They are still there, often in the shadow of my movements—faces of dust now, mingled with my solitude. I have arms that float in the crowd. The transparent crowd that proves nothing to me except that the world can exist without these anonymous lives that haunt me, these statues that never loved anyone because they didn't know how. I don't sleep. I would never forgive myself if an image of them happened to slip away. I never close my eyes.

I always let the coffee soak deep into me, like a battle uniform, before going in search of other smells. I coat myself in it, and I disappear, the way you make up coincidences so as not to be alone. I go into a shop; salesgirls scarred by solitude talk and talk. Bells tinkle. Women share costly secrets about ways to stop time. I pass. I look. I just barely brush against them. I would happily buy these illusions of beauty. I want so much to be beautiful.

I used to put myself through endless heartache about that. I imagined myself in the place of beautiful women, brought them into my dreams, went in search of cities where people can reinvent themselves, and talk, and be heard.

I remember a schoolyard. The geography of the place is still imprinted in minute detail on my retinas. The faces, though, have vanished. Little girls in blue and white. I had worries before that day. Already.

III

Her name was Christie, and she wore earrings that swayed in the night, the same way her sadness swayed in the depths of her eyes. Back then, I wasn't afraid yet. I watched men pass through her life. I knew what love was not.

One evening, she lost one of her earrings. I remember her spinning around and around in the dark, searching, already dying one of the many painful deaths that would come to her.

A waft of coffee, a flurry of movement, life rising up. I think of the sea that flowed through her, of the bruises that life inflicted on her. I see a little face that never quite emerged from the mist, a little face that lived eleven years of silence and decided, one morning, to melt into an illusion. That faded away because of Christie's absence while she struggled in unknown cities, alongside passersby without faces, without passions.

I walk through the crowds. The idea is to let life go on for just a little longer, so I can tell it. You'd recognize me by these sleeves, by this look of uncertainty. A moment of hesitation between her death and my own.

I remember. People said she was pretty. Her smiles were like curtains. She wrapped herself up in them. She opened them wide to the sun and the wind. I pick her out of a thousand faces, and out of three, with the same questions, the same regrets. She played to lose. She played to live.

The coffee is up to my eyes now. I need to find a beginning for this story. Can I? It begins with me. Despite having lived it like something shameful, I didn't see it begin. An umbrella opens in my head. Fingers holding a cigarette. Hands. Hands I'll see again twenty years later, tired hands, clinging to strangers, to illusions.

Now, I wish I could know even one of her dreams. I see her in bed. I'd rather she were making up for that under some provincial sky, in a blue South that belonged to her and that she'll never see again. She'd begun, before losing everything, by losing that memory of clear water, that earring she searched for so desperately by the light of a match, one deep-black night in Port-au-Prince.

Christie used to get the hell out of there in makeshift taxis, let herself be pawed at, groped, pour her blood into bodies that she didn't necessarily want to make live or, when she did want them to live, wasn't able to make them do it. She'd spent a lot of her life between sheets, beneath the weight of men who lied, men who breathed too hard. Time sank into her body; she was already thinking of other journeys, other dances, other silences. Life slipped through her fingers—she didn't feel it; she offered another pair of sandals to a little girl she kept in the corner of her eye. A thread on the water. A fragile cord.

On which tree, which door, had she hung one of her smiles? Which scents are still there in the old galleries without portraits, the walls without shadows, the mirrors without reflections, the memories you don't hide because you made love without loving, because you were afraid of another day, another night alone?

The coffee crept into the day like a pretense of happiness. She woke up. I watched her walking past. I watched her living.

She's far away from this hurrying crowd now. From this crowd that's afraid of everything, even of missing a flight. They don't smell the scent of the coffee and of the countless desires, of life, of ways to forget. Getting impatient. Leaving.

Someone jostles me. He smiles. A metaphor for the country's glittering sickness. For hunger. For a baby's death. For a bad dream. For the sudden leaving of the light. I turn, and the smells of Port-au-Prince come to me, and the noises of the wind. I close my eyes, I close the doors, and I think of her again, and of the island that starved her and reduced her to silence.

I think again of the photo in which she's holding out her hand. She's wearing a hat. Life as she had initially thought it would be is a burst of laughter, a hand shading her eyes from the sun, the unknown descending in blue waves over her provincial heart. *Maman* shut her away in an album. Her desperation not to lose her became a sickness; already, she was afraid of everything. Her eyes took on a deep sadness. It was a long time ago. I knew her with that sadness, that indecision, that made her so fragile. I don't look like her. I look a bit more like Christie. *Maman* spent her life between two cities and a man. A man who didn't really exist. A shadow of a man. She'd searched for treasures, searched for God; I'm almost positive she never found anything.

Christie, though . . . she created her own burst of laughter. The Atlantic was small and silent next to the big cool freshness that was her belly laugh.

I walk until my feet hurt in these airports. Searching, as I have always been.

The smell of Starbucks is its own brand. I allow myself to be drawn gently into it. Coffees and dreams to be shared at a counter with people who have different words, passengers on a plane, in a time that calls out these female first names too loudly, that brings in waves these faces creased with regret.

Christie came back to the house with strangers. They wore yellow shirts that I watched fade through miserable afternoons. The daily rice sat heavily in our stomachs, the evening porridge leaching out of us until the coming of the washed-out morning light, in that quarter built of walls and sheet metal. A quarter that never stopped watching and talking down from its ruin, down from its despair.

That quarter, caught between neglect and nastiness. I had to stay. Far longer than her, who had loved it despite everything. She'd run from end to end of it—that life buoy, like all the others she clung to despite everything, despite nothing, warping with the passage of days, miring her in a storm without memory that had always eaten away at her life. Our lives.

It was water, and the clapping of hands, and the beating of hearts, and unbeautiful music that spoke volumes of her friendships, her poor-person's flaws. Once, in a distant country, I thought of those rhythms. I was far away from Christie. I had chosen my distance. I regret it. The music rose in the rebellious July sun, and I hid my silence with a smile for the man who had walked with me two nights running in this happy-seeming city.

I miss that blue South of hers. I'm sure I didn't like the house where she spent her childhood. Now I miss it. The memory is there, sharp and clear. That living space between a kitchen and a cemetery, and wood fires, and rocks, and a steaming white coffeepot. We gazed at the cemetery, thinking that our neighbors continued to live. My brother and I would catch glimpses of tin cups, and we imagined that the dead ate and drank as they watched us go by. Now, these days, I wish that were true. I would like to keep up that illusion of life for you, far from the long roads that vanish in the distance, without the hope of having a tin cup and plate left on a gravestone in a third-world cemetery, where the people who pass by are always friends, or could have been.

IV

Christie was the last of the three sisters. Odile was the middle one, the first to leave the thankless province, and life. She'd gone in endless circles in the big miserable city, measured everything in height, made a child I never knew. A girl. She died young, they say. I don't know of what. No one talked about it. The dead in this family departed in silence. Forever.

We remained tethered to our sorrows, like horses of despair. We ran, heads bent low, wounded and silent. We shared nothing. Words lived only in our heads, or on scraps of paper. We surprised ourselves sometimes by suffering. Expressions were complaints, and we looked outside ourselves for ways to exist, to live. I hid myself away in books, lost my head over heroes of fortune late into the night, and woke in the morning with other solitudes. Terrifying and unspeakable.

What far-flung corners of the earth could accommodate these truths that we were, maybe, the only ones to know? Other places always called out to go. To leave with her sorrows. To go away with the desire to return to the silent places, to see again those maternal flatlands, knowing in advance that we would not find love there.

V

A little girl follows Christie. She senses the farewell in her infant soul. She would, maybe, have liked to speak about her fear of death, to cling to this woman who left everything, especially life. That was the day I learned what suffering meant. I don't remember if I'm holding the little girl back as she weeps and struggles. She knows already what it will take us years to learn, to understand. She hears the call of the earth. The names whose lives others will remember. If they want to, that is.

Hers isn't the path of a normal child. She's sitting on the ground; she's sad. I often hover over her sadness. One day, I give her a doll. She is happy. I'm alone; I didn't learn to love in time. I don't know how to hold back the violence that is coming toward her and will take her away. She falls down and gets up again. She tells me she loves me. I don't hear it. I don't understand this little girl who lives in the misery of solitude. She clung to a mother who took the ocean between her fingers, who went away to look for an idea of happiness.

The little girl had spent her short life losing herself in the numbers and letters you don't need to learn when you have to die at not quite twelve years old. She was beautiful, and she would stay that way. She was afraid of the old white-haired people who went by in the street and leapfrogged the painful stages to go and be the first to taste the ocean, to plunge into its blue love.

She had deepened the silence between these people who loved each other without ever talking to one another, these sisters of despair who sometimes came together in the solidarity of tears, sitting around the same memories, dreamless vestal-white virgins lying down on the damp straw of men.

The little girl was born in the blue province, in the house between the garden and the cemetery. The white coffeepot must have steamed on that day, to celebrate her birth. I was far away, and I was the same age then as she would be when she died. I imagine her watching those faces, listening to those voices, and wishing for something else. In that sea-blue landscape there was nothing alive but the fire sputtering beneath the white coffeepot and the cemetery, spreading, growing, following everyone through the dusty streets where the toothless and the shabby cross paths with young women who should have been beautiful, and ministers in search of gods.

That province didn't love me either. I feel as if it squirmed beneath the look of fear I threw it. My brother, it had loved. I kept myself apart from its sunrays, its drums, its mysteries.

I was not at home there. The little girl was born in the midst of all that, and they didn't love her. I didn't see their faces, but they can't have loved her.

I will find myself again, surely, if the way has stayed the same, if you still have to go through the little thicket, and down the path, and keep to the right where it forks, past the two small houses with straw roofs. It's baffling how this place I have always disowned is still soaked deep into my bones, haunting me even today. As if I had a debt to pay. An empty place to be filled.

The little girl was born in this godforsaken place—she was a part of it—and she had come back to it, had learned to keep her head down, to face the earth that never stopped calling out to her, that measured her steps. Through her tiny skylight she had dreamed so as not to leave too soon, to forget the failure of this family of silence, sealed up in anguish, who looked at themselves from behind in the black mirror of days marked only by a few insignificant words. Musicless days.

They had taken the little girl to church a year after her birth, on the day of her first communion, once after her first communion, and on the day of her death. The events were almost similar. Sad. The father was absent from every one of them; he had gone very early in her life to a country where they hoped he was still alive, from which he used to send cassette tapes of his voice at first. He spoke only of regret and wanted, from a distance, to keep the woman who, at first, slept with his

17

picture under her pillow. Today his memory blurs together in my head with the riots and false hopes that coursed through the streets back then. The little girl had cried on the day he left, the same way she would cry a few years later when Christie, her mother, went away. She looked like this father who had no past, no family. We had tried to issue him a past like the police issue a certificate of good conduct—another history, another departure.

They had married in the blue province. I wasn't there. My brother was.

The photos of this father with no dreams and no profession had vanished from our house. I don't know how. As easily as he had vanished himself. The cassette tapes had stopped arriving. The months went by, and the flames of her passion for him flickered out and flared back to life again like in some lowering illustration of hell.

On the day of her first communion, neither her father nor her mother was there. Some people die of far less than that. She would wear the same dress in her casket, as if she didn't need to live much longer. They were the same days, the same absences. I tried, in vain, to connect with someone as she was dying in a hospital for the poor.

Poor like the life she had just passed through very quickly, the way you move rapidly through a deserted, unfurnished place when you're in a hurry, when what lies beyond the shadow is more important. I had hands as large as the sky. As empty as her life. Even today, when I hold out those hands, I don't see anything passing through them but small, transparent, anemic clouds. I was poor and alone, looking for something new to say. Just like I am now.

The world had stopped changing, open to this page of calamity, this story without an ending. Women passed through by life and death, paths that stop at silence.

Dina has never been in that place. I envy her absences. Her confidence—or her fear—has remained the same. She has always split herself between unknowns, without question, without hope. She has slipped out of her past like an old dress. She has forgotten the curves of these streets, these tight-packed houses, these corridors where people's eyes trap you and bury you. She has conquered big cities and oblivion. There is only the shadow of the cemeteries, and the voices of two little girls, that come sometimes to trouble her nights.

The two little girls, to whom Christie gave birth in the blue province, are running, uncomprehending. They're running, like in games where you hide, where you cover your eyes to hold in the laughter and make childhood last longer. They left one morning or afternoon, without the little brother, the sole boy she had after wanting one for so long. Luck, they say, is living, no matter how, no matter the cost. There are some who keep only the past, even other people's, in case they need it someday. Like a burst of music, a road that leads everywhere.

Dina left young, under the arm of a *maman* who got the hell out of this country before anyone else. First to leave, first to die. She had grown up in a city where people are so close to death that all you have to do is breathe on them to finish them off. The lampposts of this city, where the streets sometimes pass for copies of paradise, sing an endless refrain of the blues. The women swallow up the wind of the bitter seasons, the men drowning in the earth and manufacturing dreams that, like greedy birds, bring their desire-swollen hearts back to the country each time.

VI

Airports are distillations of the world. I like thinking of them that way. The hope of leaving and the desire to come home, existing side by side. Any voyage is possible. My mind flies off toward the blue province once again. I don't know, anymore, why I always associate it with blue. It isn't even my favorite color.

To understand it, I need to walk down that long pebbled dirt path again. It's a summer day in some year of my childhood, my dress catching on the brambles. There is a man riding alone on a bicycle. A tomb faces onto the beaten-earth road, in which his wife has lain buried for a few weeks now. Women live better in memory. I look for sorrow or nostalgia in him.

Dina is with me today. She wouldn't remember. These memories would be a source of shame, a shame so acute she could die of it. Women are coming back from church. Silently, with a look, we gauge our resemblance to them, and we smile at each other. We have exiles ahead, big cities, plans. If you want it to survive, you have to nurture it early: your exile, or your flight, or your death.

The man on the bicycle is still coming. I try to imagine what she must have looked like, his young wife, lying beneath that slab. I'm too young to wonder if she loved. If she loved him.

They left to die elsewhere, Christie, Odile, and soon, perhaps, Odile's daughter Dina. Left so that they would have the right to choose their deaths. They were born here, at the end of the last war and the beginning of all wars.

I'm on a Port-au-Prince street, and I'm searching for some fragments of you, your voices, lost among these pointless cries. I'm terrified of no longer recognizing these places that are still inhabited by your hopes. My mind hasn't yet adjusted to the new concession. It's like a setting aside of your memories, a loss of citizenship.

A thousand places sleeping, a thousand places forgotten. The most beautiful dreams are the ones in which they come back, with eternity in their suitcases, like the Cubans on the other side of the sea. Cuba, which still possesses the body of one of my grandfathers who went there to work a long time ago. A story handed down like a bequest, because this family holds on to its own. The world is small; one day we'll tell it. One day we'll know.

Three women, three dramatically identical, dramatically different stories. I was happy here once. I search mechanically for the seats, the place where I was. Why hadn't I looked closely at the spot? It would have been useful today. Maman has told me about school days, the lonely path, the fear. I imagine them walking, the three sisters. Now, having learned to love them, I put them in the shoes of the schoolgirls I see passing, shifting them to another time. Nothing has changed. The steps have retained the same cadence: sad, unsure that other days can exist. Every one of these schoolgirls' peals of laughter throws in the face of the day a story without an ending, a story that is not yours.

Your words, strewn on the path for the butterflies. At Saint-Jean, they said, there were thousands of them, emerging from the same sleep, like the ones fluttering in my mind now. I saw some once, too—not in your South, but they must be related.

You made the grammar and arithmetic sing in other seasons; you learned the insignificant, what doesn't last. Death will be the only step you have ever taken into the absolute.

Voices crackling from a loudspeaker. Different voices explaining in multiple languages what we must not do, what federal law prohibits. No one seems to be listening, including me. Like in that church in the blue province where I went once.

Christie's mother and two sisters, a few years later, had changed religions, quit smoking. When she was asked to give up coffee, though, she couldn't do it. It was easier to change her religion than to stop drinking coffee.

Coffee is a ritual. Even in the cradle they give us a few drops, with peals of laughter. Each girl born into this family takes over this ritual, which stops only with death. Braziers take me back to my childhood. Starbucks is filled with the scent: a pan of beans roasted on the fire and then ground. A young girl on either side of the mortar, each with a long and heavy stick, pounding the coffee forcefully by turns. Their clothes are completely black from the dark coffee powder afterward. The brew that is prepared from this and served to everyone is strong, full bodied. I never pounded the coffee beans myself, but God, how I loved to watch.

VII

Mother came from a place that had a woman's name: Suzanne. Suzanne produced a lot of coffee, she said, and it was cold there. Even now I search for Suzanne on every map, without ever finding it. Suzanne, I am sure, is somewhere, hiding behind another name. Maybe she has changed a great deal, and maybe her coffee is no more, but Suzanne is alive inside me, a lost and forlorn child, waiting for me.

I can sense a thousand whispers in this quarter, where even the cement of the houses speaks. Life unspools here without hope. A vast labyrinth where you hide yourself, where you lose yourself. A detour by death. Everything rests on a look. Identities are in people's minds. The only law is that of pretense.

In this quarter, the concrete grew as fast as the children. Sometimes, for whole days, you saw nothing but sand. Everything was dirty white or the gray cement of death. Night came on very early, like premature old age, and you found yourself shut in. The fear of evil, of desire. A great loop that often closed again on the children. A flat refusal.

Time had left her with an accent, an accent from nowhere, without a place or a way out.

Christie was the youngest, the prettiest, they said, of this family of three daughters. I have always known Christie, because I've always wanted to look like her, to share with her those mysteries, those dreams of freedom I read in her eyes. Her pretense was so real in my eyes, her cigarette tip so bright that I floated away with her on a dream cloud.

My mother and Odile I identify by their acts, their stories, which even now linger in the realm of the serviceable, the cobbled together.

Odile had created her own world; her attentions were different, practical. By dint of leaving, she was merely a wave of the hand given out of habit. Gone from home at sixteen to Panama, and Puerto Rico, and other countries that don't inspire dreams. She'd started over from scratch. Life was out there. Death too.

Somewhere else to be born, somewhere else to think of returning. An immense thoroughfare of sand and water. Out there, she thought, life is played on a coffee table with equally matched players. Even the women take their places: single women, easy women, virgins. She belonged to the last category, according to her sisters: one of those who made love with their eyes and had no past.

VIII

America, open and weeping, welcomed Christie on a Saturday. We didn't see her again. There were rumors that the time was passing lazily for her, with a new man from time to time and small achievements here and there that made people here smile with pride.

Odile had gone away, too, with her two daughters, Dina and Rachel. It was too long ago for me to remember, really. They said Rachel, the younger one, had no heart—or, rather, the heart she had was no good. She died in a hospital, without understanding any of it, I'm sure, without memory, or reference. I don't remember the day, or the date, or the year. Neither does anyone else.

Odile spent the nights of sorrow and grief plotting the course for Christie, meant to be consulted when, in time, she followed the same path. It wouldn't do to lose one's way en route to death.

Christie left. She lived in America for ten years. She arrived there in time to bury Odile, to have children, to think with compassion of those who had stayed behind in that country with nothing to live for, nothing to hope for. That was the idea of happiness.

Odile died perhaps two or three years after Christie's arrival. Withered with memories of her broken dreams, in her forty-year-old body without a past.

No one remembers. There is no story to write. No anniversary to mark.

Odile had left one living daughter. Dina lived for herself alone, and for her freedom. Without papers and without a past, Dina fared better than anyone else. She forgot. She applied herself to the task of forgetting. The rivers of the blue province had run dry in her head, the horses she had loved, the little religious school she'd attended; today, all of that is very nearly a source of shame. She has burned it all in her mind. I think she's angry with herself for continuing to recognize the accents of her mother tongue, which she has tried a thousand times to silence around her.

I make promises to myself in this airport. Which flight to take? I am so alone, and so limited with my Haitian passport. Everyone must see me hesitating on the edge of the precipice as they pass, hurrying, pulling suitcases with a thousand secrets, suitcases full of landscapes, memories, time they can get back.

I'm wearing white and blue today. I'm certain of it. Why am I trying to fool myself by seeing my outfit as mauve and gray? Is it because of the long sleeves of this mauve sweater, maybe? The gray trousers were for no reason except that, in my head, they go with the mauve sweater. I'm tense. The time passes, like the passengers. Here, seconds matter; they are monitored and tracked. People even say time is money. Certainties are built from these seconds. Itineraries to make women in other countries dream, to create mirages. It takes true eyes to see the majesty of these airports, the hurried steps and icy smiles of these strangers.

IX

One more stopover in front of the mirrors, to see how alone we have always been. Since one particular June I have been sitting with this solitude. I take up all the space I need in this airport without asking for anything. International airports must be made for this; you pay a tax to watch people and to be alone, waiting, with a coffee.

Christie had never seen an airport. She entered this country some other way; I don't know how. She landed in a prison, a baby in her belly. That baby enabled her to stay in the country, and she'd found a place at the table. She loved it. Life is better here, anyhow; you can live, eat, be happy, die. Freedom is nothing other than this. As long as you can make it happen, and make it happen in time, like she did. Ten years in the life of a woman, ten years torn out of life despite her, despite everything.

When Christie landed in this country, she was already promised to a man. Like in the stories, and the true accounts, in old books. Her journey had been paid for in exchange for her body and her soul. The bargain was more than fair, everyone said. Misery is a hulking prison, one you don't escape without paying the price.

It's between here and there that our stories of outrage intersect. The living children of our chimeras rising up in the dark night of our sighs. If life remade itself, we would still be there, hoping for love at the end of this crossroads, an endless torment, a vast ruin. The face of our terrors would reveal itself; we are so anonymous between these sheets, so pure, so far from those hands that touch us and drag us from our sheltering innocence.

I am searching for you now to make that declaration of love and purity to you that will cleanse you of those elsewheres, those agonies. I can offer you a smile from this place against those Florida deaths, those New York injuries, those anywhere uncertainties.

In this dream, Christie was a tree. She was green, all green, all suffering. She had found time to sit between me and the page of the book I was reading. It was December. I still cry thinking about it; she is my only excuse for crying. She spoke in my dream about her absences, the violence of her path, her memory that remained. I was certain she wanted to go back home. I held her hand for a moment. It was an interrupted memory that never took up its thread again, hair down, hands that stripped the present of its meaning, threw it off track.

Blue

I feel love for us, as seen from this chair whose precise location I won't even remember the next time I travel.

Christie's children were born without identity, without roots, without customs. Elsewhere belonged to them at last. The stage wasn't set, but the actors were there. The same ambience, the same voices, the same misery. They had their heritage of misery, their ghetto. After Christie, of course, they were separated, torn apart. And I am far away from their lives, in an airport, waiting to depart. I have always been far away; I have watched everything pass by, and even now, from this chair, I continue to do the same thing. I watch so that I will forget.

Island of sighs, island of martyrs, island of lost time. Songs heal nothing. Mouths without values, words without reason. Night and day, they swallow up everything in these screamless, frightless nights. All that time spent spinning in circles. Losing yourself first. Then death.

I'm halfway through the words, halfway through the pages, halfway through the month of October. Christie is moving at breakneck speed—what an apt expression—on her way somewhere else. She'd dreamed no dreams and made no testament that day; her solitude must, surely, have been even greater than usual. The man she had married was one of those beings who will never exist. Had she ever really had a choice? She hadn't even chosen her own beauty.

Far away from her paths, her rivers, her blue province, she had found wings to change to another world, to fly away. An angel reinstated to divinity, cradled once more in whiteness.

It's a world I don't know—that's certain—that magical *elsewhere*. I have only snippets of itineraries and letters from you, lost forever, buried forever in those foreign soils. Anonymous letters, stripped bare.

X

The road to those pristine, far-flung places was long. The morning wind whipped our faces. The hope that they were on the other side of the mountain made us sing. Those healing virgins who knew of all afflictions in advance—Marie and Altagrâce and Bernadette. In the gray dawn, hundreds of women spreading out in prayer. Why couldn't the earth spin in the other direction, just once?

The Blessed Virgin, Morne Calvaire, blue, white—women, a scattering of men. Dear God, mother Mary, bring elsewhere here to us, heal us of all our words, protect us from evil. I was there in the cold morning, one vacation day. Surely. I watched. I anticipated the moment when I would finally have that little silver-colored medallion, the image of the Virgin Mary with two snippets of blue fabric and a pin, which I would wear all week until it disappeared somehow.

Time had gotten stuck somewhere here; the prayers had remained the same. The people didn't age. They passed their youth on to a child, a loved one, a relative, or they kept it until they died. The youth of dreams unrealized, the youth of those who have never known anything else, who were greeted only by the same images at the end of the road.

I watch the rain fall, a thousand fairylike drops on the tarmac. Life is beautiful when you're watching it from a distance, watching it through the window of an airport somewhere else. I imagine that it's even better when your head isn't filled with several deaths and more farewells than you know what to do with. The rain is lovely here, soft and steady. Like it was once, on the corrugated metal roof of the house on hot July evenings. Those rains, which were also sometimes storms of fury that came straight from the graves of the dead in the cemeteries, carried away children and objects and even our memories.

The first rain after Christie was fine and gentle. Florida mourns the loss of its memory. Florida mourns for the childhoods and the lost stories of the women it has watched pass through, these women it did not take the trouble to know. Those eternal guests who now sleep beneath its sheltering sky, like distant relatives who arrive for a visit one day and never leave. Even when they know they are not wanted.

I never shared very many things with them. Nor they with me. We spent our lives forgetting each other, not seeing one another. I heard your stories like fables of long ago, often mingled with tales of the blue province, of dramas and beliefs I allowed myself to find bizarre. Now I am searching for my similarities to you. I missed you somewhere, like that passenger who has just missed her flight. Yet I knew your paths; I had reference points for you, and even some memories.

The day's colors blend, and I have a distant love who will not return from a trip to New York. Another death to mourn. Another desire to bury with them, with the others. It's the dead season. The season of the dead. I'm alone in a foreign airport—I have sleeves that flop past my wrists like soft, helpless hands—in an almost mob waiting to board. I don't want to go back; I'm afraid of meeting my mother's eyes again in Port-au-Prince. I remember your lessons of beauty, which my mother never learned.

Dear Maman, I'm afraid to see you now. I'm embarrassed to explain things to you that have no explanation. That means, probably, that you shouldn't look at me, or try to understand me. Dear Mother, with your strange, sorrowful eyes, I would have been so beautiful if I'd looked like you. I don't look like anyone, really. Not even myself. I've changed my skin and my convictions too many times, too many different shoulders, too many different loves.

I am a bearer of news. I am afraid. I refuse your heritage of drudgery and servitude and age-old solitude. I refuse your sad looks, your resignation, your fear.

I see again that defaced city, without song, without all of you. Maybe you didn't even exist. Does the civil status registry remember you? That city without memory, bleached and faded by the rain.

I have retained the friendship of certain paths sealed up in the scent of the night, surreal poison disseminated in the eyes of passersby. I come back in silence, to tell the story between passion and despair, to paste a Floridian street over a path in the blue province, a rutted road in a quarter in Port-au-Prince. I, who am neither magician nor alchemist; I, who have no talent.

How do you tell a story you don't know? I, who have always kept my history separate, convinced that life is short and that each person must tell their own story—I will have to tell one now. I must tell it, tell it to the end.

Their past, their history, their future stayed on their hands, nothing but spots and stains acquired in hotels and kitchens, selling their time for almost nothing, to preserve the slightest dignity in a country that should, perhaps, have been compared to the blue province—you never know. It's true that they had never known life here. They didn't know it anywhere else, either, in the end: life as they had imagined it, a life with plans and self-reflection, perhaps, and reflection on others. Life with different, and rather similar, tomorrows.

XI

I'm coming back from a trip. I'm coming back from the end of a story. There are people for whom one country isn't enough to lay out their tragedy, a tragedy that has played out in silence, on the flip side of our days and our desires.

One more pause in this space where the rain separates me from your questions. A lush and gentle rain. I lose myself in it, forgetting this weighty present and that past I have been trying to reassemble for years, for days. What is my mother thinking about right now? My mother with her eyes full of things unsaid, gazing out into the blackout of her quarter. That quarter she has worn like a garment for thirty-five years.

For thirty-five years she has said her morning and evening prayers there. Three children who carry the same name—three children who took their character and their troubles from the examples of others; they, too, learned to create silence beneath a roof where no one spoke of love, where love in a neighbor's house was criticized, dismissed, doubted, distorted. Love was bad. Especially for a girl. Love was a practical exercise: it took persistence to succeed at it. You began at a specific age and did the same thing all your life. Built your routine and made sure it lasted.

My heart is in shreds, and soon it will be time to board, to fly toward all that exhaustion, that diminution, that island whispering low in the backyard of the northern dwellers with their festering, their evil eye.

I am on the trail of old loves, of love letters sent by mistake, of unique, towering tragedies. Macabre games of liberty. The day is hesitating between blue and gray. Death couldn't have wished for anything better than this pathos, this normality shot through with anguish. Mid-October of a year to stay at home, a television year, a year in which fiction revolts. In mid-October 2001, I am dreaming illegally in a Florida airport. People have traded their hurried Western approach for one that is heavy, measured, compliant, antiterrorist. I set up my story like a tent, at my own risk, my own peril.

Death is everywhere. I cannot claim solitude in my suffering. Every television station is showing people weeping, lamenting. Fire and planes and ash. Especially ash. All the world's so-called citadels, its strongholds, are nothing but houses of cards, sandcastles, waiting to entomb bodies and memories.

I am as far away from New York as I am from the blue province. The maps have blurred together. In the space of a moment, the disasters have merged. How death always looks the same! The loudspeakers are broadcasting threats. Everyone is afraid. I'm afraid too. At security just now, they went through all my clothes. I felt my whole body rebelling. I stayed silent. I couldn't have spoken anyway. For a week now I have been on strike from feelings, on strike from words, despite myself. My expressions boil down to two tears that slide down my cheeks, or bursts of rage at the most trivial things. Death makes me ashamed, in reality. I am ashamed when I lose someone, ashamed to say it, ashamed to feel the grief.

XII

Travelers have to be visibly honest and innocent these days. Open books. I've always hated that expression, like I hate all clichés. Eternal truths. Dogmas. But they're what make the world go round. No one sees me in my margins, my margins of error and solitude. Travelers hardly dare to breathe in these North American airports.

I've just performed my dance, with much good faith, partnered by these men in gloves, wearing masks of disdain for travelers of all races who might be terrorists or anti-imperialists. Carriers, probably, of all sorts of dreams. Prohibited, in any case. I'm traveling light, like I always do, poor and without pretension, with a ticket paid for by my father. A ticket to go and weep over a coffin on behalf of everyone, all those people who don't even dare apply for a visa for this America that is ever more hermetic, more brutal, this America where towers fall, this America suddenly seized by death like a first spell of vertigo.

I was in this airport, which occasionally took on the air of a grand promenade, a place far from my rutted roads and my smashed pavements, and I fluttered around my life like a stupid fly, soon to fall without attracting anyone's attention.

Exile, flight, misery, and humiliation are all you earn at the end of the adventure. No bright and shining light, certainly, except rarely, for a few. Life stretches away over vast fields of tomatoes and other fruits I don't know. The false sense of well-being has convinced everyone, even the ones who say they want to go back after a while. I came to understand this vast Floridian South very quickly, welcoming and inhuman, with light to hide its ugliness, an El Dorado for millions of Haitians and Mexicans and Puerto Ricans. Widely separated neighbors, together for days in the fields and entrenched at night in their particularities, each emphasizing their dissimilarities, or their superiority, at every opportunity. It depends on who's judging.

Silence is everywhere in this huge southern land. The English is chewed-up pidgin for needs of primary communication. No efforts to be friendly in the America of differences, the America of those who get up early and go to bed late, the America of everyone, the America of poor people's dreams, the America of those who live fast and are just passing through.

A thousand lives, a thousand faces, a thousand reasons in this airport. Maybe someone is looking at me, someone with a story of his own. I would like for this to be a love story, a living story, a story about happy people. People aren't born with exile here; they don't even take the time to understand world geography. They are in the world, and they have plenty of airports, plenty of ports and platforms for those who want to come and see the world, the world they built. I would very much have liked a love story just now, someone in whose body I could spend long hours and talk, even about current events.

I was in a story without the memory of love and which would not resign itself to ending. It fed on all sorts of infidelities and unhappinesses and exploded on some mornings in reproach and despair. On the night of the bad news that would make me come to this American South, he was there, caring and generous, as he had always been. I cried the way he would have liked me to cry for him: present, alive, and in love. We had already accumulated plenty of empty evenings, close and distant; we went out and bored one another in restaurants and then in front of the television. I double-locked myself away, and I was sure he was there behind the door, waiting for me, gently appreciating my perfume and my fingerprints. He will be there when I arrive. I want him to be.

I make another trip to Starbucks. It's different from my grandmother's mountain coffee, it's true. She had the first name of a country. Argentine.

Argentine never had any horizon but the mountains. Her eyes, made blue by some miracle of interbreeding, never saw an airport, never saw so many serious people hurrying, wrapped up in their Westernness. All those people who are right even before the question is asked.

I have vague memories of a path on the edge of a river, of a market. Smells have stayed with me more than sights. Except for the image of Argentine, her long hair hidden beneath a scarf, holding the bridle of a donkey on whose back she let me ride at daybreak. She was standing there, in that tide of indefinable odors, and I had the impression that dozens of hands were reaching out for her. I should have wept for her on that day, wept for her approaching death, because you don't live like that. She had chosen her coffee, her poison, disregarding the opinions of the doctors, those slick and clever men she always eyed suspiciously, she who had for so many years preferred the direct language of the *loas* and the *houngans*.

It was unequivocally a death ritual: large white tin cups with a single red-and-green flower painted on the outside, just women sitting around a wood fire, and the coffee poison, syrupy and brown, carefully drunk down to the grounds. I'm in that setting again, coughing by the wood fire, and I'm eight years old, and I am letting my soul out for a walk among this female humanity.

Now I let the same aroma penetrate deeply into my thirty-year-old body, leaning on the counter of the little coffee bar in this airport in this rainy mid-October. My overlong sleeves make it hard to hold the paper cup of cappuccino. Would Argentine have liked this coffee with the exotic name? My sleeves are like my life. Overstretched, overflowing. I am far from the seasons of my childhood and yet buried up to my neck in a past stitched together from snippets and scraps.

A civilization of silence also means carpets for walking on, dark glasses for pretending not to see. Not to look back, especially. I am not part of that civilization. I was born like those women, in the brutal backwardness that jerks people from that part of the world out of sleep, makes them double-lock their doors so no one will get in. I will never be above all suspicion of backwardness. None of those women will. Not even Dina, though she seems to have managed to forget.

The Floridian South walks and dances, like me, to orphan notes. If I could only undo those misbegotten knots that tie me to that part of the world I have long regarded only as a sort of carnival, where I go for a brief moment of amusement. Without obligation or even great desire. I have three bodies that sleep there today, and I am playing out a part of my tragedy to indifferent spectators. In an airport.

Without silence, the spectacle would be appalling. I perform my number alone. A tragic solo. I cling almost desperately to my cardboard cup, my coffee that is turning cold like the promises of life and returning I have sometimes made. I don't remember what day it is. That would be surplus information anyway. I already know what the weather is, and where and in which country I am, and to which country I am preparing to return, and I know, more than anything, that my life will never be the same again.

I don't remember much about myself. I grew up blurred, submerged in a flood of impairments. I went through my childhood at a run, with the image of an authoritarian father and a silent, fearful mother. Twenty years in the void, with no reference point, no memory, no self.

It was once me and never quite me, in this cobbled-together quarter, shut up in my own ordinariness, in my differences. Invisible. The paths to school had been the same for forty years, and the only different people were two poets, old in my eyes, and mysterious. Their names were René and Jean-Claude, and they had spent their lives collecting legends, gathering a treasure trove of all types. From Grande'Anse to Port-au-Prince by way of the sea, they had even brought back the billows and the waves and the cries of the tormented, tombless drowned.

From Monday to Sunday, from behind the metal gate that held me prisoner, I reimagined the scenery of that street where people went back and forth, talking loudly, louder than their misery, louder than their despair. In the evening, prayers reached my ears. Loud noises to combat oblivion. People laughing uproariously, crying out. God didn't hear. I knew he didn't hear. I kept my eyes open as wide as the night, and every once in a while I heard the sound of shots. The makers of death setting about their task wholeheartedly. That was the era of the military, of one coup after another, of empty streets.

Doors stayed closed, as if that could keep them out. Lists of corpses found on the pavements overnight were read out on the radio each morning. Massacres of peasants at Port-de-Paix and Jean-Rabel, with all the profane vulgarity claimed sometimes by absurdity and always by ignorance.

The poets seemed to have the gift of speech, more beautiful than my own, that you could listen to with your eyes closed. I became someone when I stepped beyond the boundaries of this quarter. My life was cracked in two, divided between silence and the pages of a few books with, on their back covers, tragic-faced poets I came to see as father and God. They held the only truths worthy of being listened to and followed.

I would like to believe that I was a rebel when I think of myself back then, but I would be deliberately fooling myself. I prefer to see myself as a cheater, a fourteen-year-old girl who created two lives for herself, who inhabited the skin of two irreconcilable individuals. When I was outside my home, I lived out loud, and I was real in that life.

My notebooks came with their pages already yellowed. Cheap notebooks, undoubtedly, notebooks that wore out fast. I wrote the passing time in them, and mathematical formulas. When afternoon fell on the words of the teachers who took their turns one by one in these overheated classrooms, and whom I found mostly stupid, I went to find the poets, or their shadows. Free words, words offered, with the taste of forbidden fruit. Words to be thrown in the face of my quarter when

I finally made the leap out. Words to cover the faces of my parents and the radio.

They were all trying to find themselves in that house. My brothers, my father. My mother didn't exist. She had accepted her nonexistence; she was sometimes the echo of my father, whom everyone in the quarter addressed as *sir*. My father never let anyone forget that he had studied with the friars, that he worked in an office, that he could write and do sums. He adored his public. The men and women who came to listen to him. He scrambled everything. He claimed titles that he didn't have. My brothers and I endured his mechanical love, his whippings, his rages.

Now, Maman listens to the priests, the ministers. She will always find someone to listen to. I imagine she has pain sometimes; I prefer not to look closely. I know she goes back, occasionally, to her blue province where the rivers, I'm told, have killed themselves, dried up. I, who have no place to go back to, except toward the danger, the silences—toward the whiteness, and the fading.

XIII

The Church of Saint Paul. Or perhaps some other saint. She was lying almost across the doorjamb, mimicking a sleep that frightened me. That sleep they called death. A little boy of four was crying with all his heart and all his incomprehension at that pristine, perfect sleep. That must be true rest. The kind you have to deserve.

Saint Paul and his songs. An ordinary Saturday in the life of the world. A humanly ordinary event. People who don't carry much weight in the history of the world. I wanted to see Christie's last journey, her last path. It was a long asphalted ribbon, very straight, with white dashes down the middle and trees all around. Beautiful trees. Very green. It was like heaven. Maybe it was heaven. Two white crosses planted in the wind as a reminder that two people had stopped here to watch their lives flash past and be reconciled with space.

To yield up the spirit. What an appropriate expression! To yield up her spirit, to divest herself of her memories, to extinguish the flames of her body, just like that, one morning, by accident. In this church, Saint Paul or some other saint, we were death, and I was in an unevenly matched fight with time—time, without a soul and without a schedule, and I, who was demanding that time promise the past and the present, begging for the impossible. I wanted to, I could, give everything. From the extremely precious to the most banal. My sincere declarations of love. My stolen images, and even my random ones, like that little girl at the Pétion-Ville market with one damaged eye. Maybe the heart too.

Our mutual birthplace, remember, I said to it, sometimes provides images that linger on life like rancid oil. We were already guilty of our own deaths. We had all fallen like coins but without noise, without surprise. There remain of us, in the archives of some schools, a few erasures, silent blemishes intimidated by the shelves full of books we have never opened.

I turn my gaze again toward that other quarter, where you found yourself once. Infidelity is one of life's natural behaviors. A gritty slum on a mountainside; from a long way away you could see the cement blocks crowded together, children trudging with pails, going to fetch far-distant water. A quarter to which you had traveled for some love or desire for freedom I can't remember. It doesn't matter; it lasted only a few months, just long enough for a breakup or an overdose of solitude.

I often make a pilgrimage to our places of solitude. All of Port-au-Prince dims in my mind then. We are deaf and mute, inventing a tangent on which to meet, a bridge that will link multiple spaces, multiple lives. Quarters, mingled people, words, paths all leading to this airport in a northern country, far from the rivers and watercourses of the blue province that created travel sickness, washing childhood out to a miserable white.

The *loup-garous*, the wolf men that we were told should have entered the house with the straw roof in the blue province and changed our destinies, were never able to do it. I had always believed they lived in the adjacent cemetery and that they were merely the unquiet dead. That was what my grandmother told me, but there were also so many other things my mind still has never been able to comprehend.

The bodies of our old dolls flung away into the fields became zombies: ghastly, malevolent beings that ate children, caused all sorts of diseases, and wiped out the harvests. I would have happily offered myself up to a werewolf if the story hadn't already been too far along, and then I wouldn't be sitting in this airport in this month of October, listening to threats coming from a loudspeaker. Threats in all languages. Worse than the threat of werewolves in that southern province. That blue province, sometimes with hints of gray.

I remember two visits to the blue province. It's labeled Gros-Marin on the map of Haiti. There must be other names that I don't recall. I loved that long road trip, the names of the towns and villages we stopped in—it was like a dream. Maman had even promised, the first time we went, that we would stop at a place called Carrefour Des Ruisseaux—Crossroads of the Streams. I didn't see any streams there, or even a crossroads, but the coconut palms bending so lovingly toward the sea were worth all the other beauties hoped for and denied.

This was a South jealous of its sun, the South that had watched my mother and her sisters grow up, kissing my lips with a warm breeze. I was wedged uncomfortably into my seat on the bus, and I tried to hide my dreams from Maman, who never stopped blaming me for not resembling her. The journey unfurled slowly, like my life in this airport. The bus would stop at Cavaillon, and then, via a road made of pebbles, we went on to Gros-Marin. One of the trips was for the pleasure of seeing Grandmother and Grandfather. The other was to bury Grandfather.

I didn't get to see that sweet old gentleman who spoke only rarely. We'd arrived too late. I have forgotten the timbre of his voice. He hadn't set foot outside his home village until he was already very old. It was an event. He read softly, just for himself. His voice didn't carry. He must have been unhappy all his life. He was tyrannized by his wife, my grandmother, with the silent complicity of his daughters. They took turns letting out great howling wails on that day, even though they had encouraged him to die, even though he had already been buried a long time ago beneath tons of silence.

That was my last trip to Gros-Marin. I was thirteen. When I dared to tell those women they didn't have the right to cry,

I'm sure one of them wished me dead alongside Grandfather. That was what always happened in this family after someone died. You had to die to earn the right to be loved.

Grandfather had joined his lifelong neighbors in the adjoining cemetery, his companions in silence. His cane remained, and his old man's clothes, and an old book, and his daughters and a wife he surely did not love or whom he must have stopped loving. It was a long time ago.

Outside her own home, though, she was human, Grannie. That's what we called her. We talked about her with tenderness when she was far away. Her children's children, including me, believed she could heal our fevers and our bouts of flu, protect us from werewolves, win wars for us. And there was truth in it. She prepared potions for us and gave us massages with oil of Palma Christi, the secret of which she alone possessed, we thought. After her death, I longed for years for the taste of her healing tisanes in my mouth, for the sight of the purple fruits she brought from Gros-Marin with love. Surely.

She died on December 10. We'd been getting word for two months that she wasn't well, that she'd broken her arm. Maman went to see her every now and then, until she died. On that day I was supposed to recite René Philoctète's poem "Mes Camarades de Soleil" onstage at the Rex Theater. I, like René's friends, played the games heartbroken children play.

Odile was already dead in Florida. Christie, who I have just seen in her coffin, couldn't come back into the country because she didn't have a visa. My mother, the oldest and the least resourceful of the daughters, was all alone at her mother's funeral. Everyone mourned in their own solitude. But you had to choose. Christie had already chosen. A year earlier, when her child had died, she hadn't come back. She had, once again, chosen to experience from far away her mother's move to the other side of the family estate.

There remained only the thousands of kilometers of solitude to share. No one was alive. No one believed they could get out. Death was the only choice. At least it didn't demand complicated explanations. It seemed to me like I was seeing false grief everywhere, public displays.

This morning I am measuring the steps of those people, my people, their lowly paths. I am seeking their souls to console myself. I have an urgent need for reasons to dream, to continue to watch travelers, to think of where they might be going, what their lives are like. I'm alive, too, with roots painfully severed. I am strangely alive.

XIV

The perfume of the mirrors follows me. I don't belong to anything. Realization of disaster. I can't go far with my deaths and my history in tatters. I can hear the call of my city so strongly: thirty years living the same despairs, clinging together, breaking our backs to create mornings and evenings in which to grow old. I still love its appearance of nowhere, that whole treasure of obsolescence we have together.

I can hear the sobbing of the mirrors that have sent back their reflections of this fateless place a thousand times. I can detect the fingerprints of the passersby and poets who have closed this door that groans, sometimes, when it is opened to the dawn. And that never keeps its promise. I have gone around and around the image, walking in the same direction as the crack in it, and this afternoon I am cold in this airport seat. My solitude makes waves whose foam wets my feet, my hands, my eyes.

The mirrors' laughter has broken thirty years of life, thrown into chasms all of the complaints disguised as gladness.

Time, and others, have given titles to these gestures without pretention, except that of making us turn our backs on one another because we have missed the first kiss and the final word of love. Like a traveler misses her flight, waits, and catches another because she absolutely must leave. Must go back, to somewhere.

Go back to the country. Revisit her old places. Her old habits. Like complicit garments that give the impression of a second skin. I will always be lived in by these places from another time, this feeling of things unfinished since my failed emergence from childhood.

None of us had any memory, any past. We lived in a quarter that exhaled an odor of life and immediacy that was almost convincing. We all passed through without leaving a trace; we never experienced pride. Every hour was the same, and we dampened our senses to catch every feeling that passed. You could even follow the trail of smoke. Afternoon was the time for large fires. We burned misery up in them, and everyone vanished behind transparent curtains. We could even believe ourselves happy.

Everything had always been worn out in this quarter. The houses, the trees, the cars, the people, the dogs. Some mornings began with women's dresses. They didn't understand. They found themselves naked and more fragile in the face of these men, these children, these dry faucets. They closed the doors of their houses that opened onto the yard, ashamed of their misery. They were, without knowing it, public servants being subjected to terror that stole first their voices and then their hearts. And so they bent their steps toward the churches, clinging, as if to a lifesaver, to a Bible they never read, that most of them could not read.

It was a ghetto. I was there. I passed through it. With my childhood, my fumbling dreams, and I kept my voice low, the way I still do today. The women looked at themselves in half-broken mirrors. The mirrors were framed in all colors; I remember yellow and red in particular. Can you see yourself as beautiful in a broken mirror? I would like to know. They hid behind doors and windows to do their hair, and put on clothes, and watch themselves disappear.

The lady who lived across the road from my mother always left her door open. Aside from the bed and the table in the single room, she had a large mirror, and everyone in the street could look at themselves in it as they passed. At a certain time of day, the reflected light was blinding. The mirror was white and indiscreet. I never saw myself in it. I was too far away. I regret that. It would have changed my life. I am sure of it. I would have chosen my path earlier. The mirror broke on a Monday. I don't know how. It was an accident. And then the whole quarter was without a reflection.

The neighbor lady spent years talking about her mirror, which she never replaced. I'll bet she's still talking about it, more than twenty years later. I can't think about the quarter without remembering her mirror. She was a Protestant, like most of the people in that ghetto. Maybe that's why she never replaced the mirror, why she allowed all those beautiful reflections to be lost, those prettified reflections, those illegal moments of passion snatched in passing at the end of the day despite the smoke.

I wasn't conscious of my flights, not yet. No one left that place; I know that now. It's those walls that I still recognize in the guitars that accompany me. It's those voices singing of this dying country. It's those peals of laughter that become will-o'-the-wisps on the nights when life faces away from me.

I have more looks than names. A whole living album of looks, enough to carpet this airport with, from floor to ceiling. Looks that came from everywhere, a whole country and its devastated landscapes, its cemeteries, its exiles. They all ached for another place. New York, Florida, Guyana, the Dominican Republic. I saw helmeted motorcyclists arriving every day with money and poorly written letters and then sometimes the children leaving, dressed in blue, crying. I knew that was the end, that I would never see them again, and I never have seen any of them again. Everything fell gently asleep; everything faded from memory.

Love didn't exist, I said to myself at those moments. My father always said that love was the worst of all catastrophes. He thought women were the great losers in love. I believed him, and until very late in my adolescence, I thought it would be better to be a man. Just as my mother must have believed, or still believed, and just as her sisters believed until they died.

This airport was the place of life, these routes thought out and traced, these established laws, these safeguards against terrorism, noisemakers, and even machismo. All of it mirrored in the souls of millions of people just a few kilometers, a stone's throw away.

My body stirred like the earth of this Floridian cemetery, a foreign trembling, a regret. The sky wept on my behalf, wetting the tarmac. The planes took off every now and then, their bellies swollen with dreams and anxieties, with future hero martyrs, how America and the world loved them. I could have wept like the sky, if not for my good faith as a bearer of bad news. Everything kept blurring in my head. I was no one specifically. I had a southern mind mixed with a poor neighborhood and a blue province buried amid untrustworthy geography, like a piece of writing that is fading away, that you have to strain to make out.

I hadn't been hungry or thirsty for a week. I was the universal inheritor of the scent of coffee; it is my memory. My present. A scent as an identity, a scent as a path to travel in order to come back. Everything was stage dressing in this country, a setting that was not mine. A stage set in an immense void in which you could hear nothing but the voices of windows open on wedges of sky, billowing tops to keep out the cold, the fear, the vanity.

I haven't retained anything on this trip but the lasts. Last bus, last dress, last tears—faces, the last time.

A little girl from another time has left traces in my movements—an unfinished dance, a fixed image, like in a photo whose paper has aged. When will the end of that dancing movement come? When will I free this suspended grace and become light, shrug off the present, and fly away to live? That little girl has a half smile too. A smile that does not dare. Barricaded. A smile with ambitions to be a full-throated laugh, full of wildness. The laughter would have burst out if someone had told her of a city like this, or another, where people are too intelligent to look one another in the eye, too intelligent to love twice.

My paper cup seems to have been drained of its soul; its coffee is cold and indifferent, and it is not black. It's a cappuccino. It doesn't even have a scent anymore, or its scent is far away, like those bodies lost in the northern maelstrom, their only baggage their own despair.

XV

My mother's heart makes the same sound as her sewing machine, which I have known my whole life. It's older than my brothers and me. Its brand is a woman's first name: Linda. It has always looked like a museum piece. All of my little-girl dresses came from beneath her magical needles that broke sometimes. I've seen many women from this family sitting behind that machine, which makes an ancient mechanical noise like Maman's heart, like the heart of all women who have been poorly loved.

Odile sat behind that machine once; it's the only clear image I have of her in my memory, sewing who knows what and singing a very popular, very sexist song by some *compas* band. Her face was serene. She was already living partly in North America and partly on the island. That gave her a kind of superiority. She had plans.

The room was filled with all sorts of objects, ugly, motley, useless. It was so crowded it was hard to move around. These sisters had nothing in common except for a physical resemblance, and their way of always acquiescing to the badly brought-up men who were their husbands. They had no heroes, no models. They were mothers. The word was synonymous with servitude and self-sacrifice.

They were together that day, all three of them, these daughters of the blue province. Their three lives gathered together in one room weren't enough to make a story. They knew of no other drink but coffee. Coffee in different cups. As different as they were themselves. Masked, veiled in coffee black, they would have been magnificent as widows, lit up by all sorts of temptations, besieged by desires, unfamiliar shivers running through them. They would keep sealed in silence all trespasses, all those acts that cannot be transformed into words, so private and illegal and tender are they.

The rumble of the sewing machine filled the room. Its motor belt running fast. It was dark and magnificent and almost enviable in its mechanical life, turning out shoddy products. It could have sewn nice ones, but a sewing machine doesn't dream alone. One by one, they put their feet on the pedal, and the long line began stretching away, the thread of dashes on the cloth joining the pieces of fabric together.

It was a kind of magic. They were happy with the results, cutting with the pretty pair of silver-plated scissors that were also older than any of the family's children. That pair of scissors cut paper, too, unbeknown to my mother, who would have been furious if she'd seen us using her treasure for that.

Children weren't supposed to touch the sewing machine, or the scissors.

I've seen sewing machines that looked like the ones belonging to other women in the quarter, but none ever looked like Linda or had a woman's name like hers. She wasn't the most beautiful, but she was unique. She had been built to withstand time, like her owner, to watch others pass through and go away, even the youngest ones. She outlived Maman's two sisters. The other machines in the quarter were white and made almost no sound.

Being a seamstress was work for poor girls. Hundreds of young girls took sewing lessons from wicked teachers. I would watch them go by in the afternoon, recognizing them by the long graduated rulers that stuck out of their bags. Slats, they called them. Courageous and resigned, the vast majority of them never became seamstresses. Never became anything. They had only taken a few afternoons out in their bags, bringing back the lingering, nasty smell of men as they went home at nightfall after sewing class.

Trends change. Now they wear white stockings even in the hottest weather, the young girls in Maman's quarter; they want to be health care workers. But they get the same miseries as always, the same solitudes, except they have lost the music of the sewing machines.

My older brother learned to operate Linda, but I never did. She is still enthroned in the house, still in use. She makes the dresses my daughter wears every year on her birthday, to please Grandmother more than anything.

My mother sits down at Linda to listen to that lovely imitation of her heartbeat when she doubts her own existence. She sits there more and more often these days, producing old-fashioned, outmoded dresses and blouses and skirts for herself that make me smile.

When I disembark at Port-au-Prince, I will go directly to find my mother, with the same desire I had to run away twenty years ago, and I will see her sewing machine set up on the porch, as if to welcome guests and old age. Linda's grim appearance will testify that passion has never lived in this house set deep in a poor quarter of squat, colorless concrete blocks.

The quarter of my childhood produces more dashed lines than Linda. People's movements are stuttering. The concrete has grown and spread. The smallest bit of empty space has been invaded. The faces have changed. People are dead or disfigured. My mother's left-hand neighbor, who knew me my whole life and always reproached me for not having enough hair, has died of an illness whose name none of her children or anyone else in the quarter could ever manage to pronounce: Alzheimer's. The true incarnation of the devil. The last time I saw her, she had even forgotten that I'd never had long hair, forgotten what a serious problem it was. She didn't recognize me in her little iron bed with her long white hair that said she was already dead. She always dyed her hair black, religiously. She thought that to be alive, you had to have long black hair.

I don't know the new left-hand neighbors. The place has new owners now, and the little pink-and-green house has been transformed into a concrete monster that casts a shadow over my mother's house. It used to be inhabited by women who spent their time shouting at one another and being shouted at by other women who claimed they were taking the women's husbands.

That was the word they used. *Taking.* That was how they expressed themselves, and the men enjoyed seeing these women go after one another when they weren't beating them themselves. They had eventually died, these women, of illnesses linked to the permanence of these false, scattered, calculated loves. I liked their obliviousness, their scorn for established, so-called correct things. They were not approved of, and people lowered their voices when they talked about them, the same way you did when you talked about politics back then, government things, forbidden things.

I had quickly discovered that there were hundreds of quarters in the capital. Quarters like catacombs. Quarters that sprang up already old, shriveled, like prisons people chose to enter. Places where God is the best-known and most indifferent figure. Pleaded with from morning to night, he is always there on the doorstep, but he never comes inside. He is sorry about all the misfortunes, of course.

Those quarters were all the same, always with a room for rent into which crowded whole families, including cousins and distant relatives. People moved from one to another. On Saturday nights, preferably. You could watch little vans arriving, crammed with old mattresses and other cheap furniture, ugly and worn out. They rented these rooms for six months or a year and then vanished into Port-au-Prince's labyrinth of streets.

I used to go through one of these quarters to get to Odile's house. A corridor, an anthill. The street was always filled with hundreds of people. It was an insomniac quarter. Alcoholic. A market and a dwelling place at the same time. And all along that corridor street, dozens of other corridors led off to unimaginable houses lived in by an incredible variety of wildlife.

At sunrise, dozens and dozens of coffee sellers would set up their stalls for the early-morning workers, most of them on their way to building sites. The coffee was prepared on small coal stoves that were dragged down the small corridors before the sun came up, raising a long trail of sparks. Like lost stars distorted by the dreams of these women who put the night-black coffee in the pots to produce that unbearable scent.

I didn't know the word *ghetto* back then, but these were ghettos. They turned their backs and grew far from prying eyes, in the purest solitude. I could sense the thousands of voices, the thousands of cries behind those walls, and I hurried through quickly, as everyone did. I knew dreams could not grow in a place like that. How fast did you have to run to get out in time, to avoid meeting one of those blank, unresponsive gazes resigned to its own misery?

Odile's house was hemmed in. It seems that, before this, she had lived in a quarter called Cour du Cimetière, which was where she had conceived and lost her first child. I can still see that tight-squeezed little house with its terrace, its two rooms, the sound of her voice, the doors open onto nothing. Odile never claimed ownership of anything here: not her paths, or her voice, or the quarters she lived in, or the houses, or her family. Nothing. No one missed her when she left; she had never been here. Her death was insignificant news, to me at least. This greatest of all absences had simply confirmed that she wouldn't be coming back again.

You have the time to watch your history unspool, sitting in an airport chair. The entire accumulation of images and feelings, failures, the long dance around nothing. No one to see. A story without witnesses is worthless, or nearly so.

The coffee is cold. I'm going to take the time to get a fresh cup, to walk this way again. The walls seem very far away. I feel small here. Everything is large in this country. It absorbs me. I am already imagining the return and my reintegration into those shrunken spaces, those dirty, cluttered streets, my nervousness when I disembark. Powerless in the face of those swarms of people, the endless clamor, the impression that no one loves anyone. All those people and their dreams of leaving, of landing one day on this runway made wet by a fine October rain.

No one speaks around the coffee bar. A silent transit of travelers hurried and unhurried, like me, with my overlong sleeves and my fear of going back, of seeing again, of telling.

I don't know how to tell things. The cashier brings a semblance of a smile to my face. I pass the perfume shop again. People look despairing, hopeless in shops. There aren't many shoppers now, since the events of September 11. It was only a month ago, after all. You have to be careful. The TV channels are still endlessly replaying images of those runaway planes smashing into the towers in New York, and everyone is wondering what the next target will be.

I'm trying to find the way that feels best for me to tell it, to say, into the silence, how I went one Saturday afternoon into a little church in the south of America—I, who never went into churches anymore. How I sat down in front of a coffin, and how a four-year-old child next to me screamed at the unhearing body. That would only be the end of the story, in any case. And the end of the story isn't good for anything. I want to scream the silences, all these pages of silence, that lost earring in the Port-au-Prince blackout, those parentheses in dark glasses, and the words I had chosen to hold back for thirty years.

That photo exists. It's in an album in my mother's house. A photo showing an unfinished gesture, a gesture tossed into the infinite, uncertain days to make up for the lack of love, of tenderness. A gesture to trivialize the departure of the father and mother, to soften the brutality of those images of coffins, of unwelcomed lives poorly lived, of legacies and regrets.

I am ashamed of my flights, my escapes. I left early and quickly, into pages, into other streets, hands over my eyes so as not to see and as much jazz as possible in my ears so as not to hear. I know the hallmarks of these flights: the full ashtray; the books; the closed doors; and, today, this airport and its blue carpets; the smell of this coffee, which is perhaps like the smell of the blood I have received; and those voices; those first names; those cries echoing in my head.

Our history before this month of October was so muted, like the silent marshes of the blue province where, once and maybe still, those lives and those purple flowers grew, whose shades are mingling now with these blue carpets, these black chairs, and my gray trousers.

When one emerged from those humid gardens—those *marshes*, as they called them—the whole weight of the sun fell on us, as if to take its vengeance at not being able to penetrate the wilderness. I walked next to Grannie's donkey. I dreamed, too, of an elsewhere that wasn't North America and wasn't the city either. An elsewhere far away from all of you.

At this precise moment I am taking my faithlessness, my inconstancy, my lack of respect out for a walk. My present is in reverse. A morning stroll in an unfriendly, distrustful airport.

I would gladly hold in my arms, if I still could, that stagnant water, that sun.

We are all connoisseurs of exile, then; we have each, individually, forged our own. To leave at any price and, for various reasons, to go far away from our roots, to make for ourselves other loves, other beliefs, and then return to the desert, to those places that have never heard declarations of love.

My solitude is denser, thicker than these marshes in which we left our traces. All my images of Christie are from behind. Heartbreak, standing out against the dawn. A woman with reasons to weep and who did not weep, who reached out for each day with both hands until that morning when America opened wide its undertaker's arms.

Returning was supposed to be a great celebration, seeing the others again and displaying her pride at having crossed the sea, at having made it to America, without ever mentioning the miseries, the uncertainties, the coldnesses, the infinite solitude of those foreign landscapes. The whole story had already been imagined, already been lived. The obligatory passage would be this airport—without the Starbucks coffee, of course. That wasn't worthy; it didn't speak the language of conviviality, the language of clenched fists with a few notes of hatred and madness.

I've never gone to see the coffee of your mountains. I've never taken the time to listen to the music of your rivers. Never absorbed your childhood myths. I am an absolute stranger. A poor inheritor of your beauty, lost to me forever. My mother was right: I don't look like her. I have been searching my soul for more than an hour, while my mind and body wandered in this airport, for some regret, and I haven't yet truly found any.

I have a kind of sick burning in my head. The same way I used to feel when I sensed myself being watched through the makeshift fence around my grandmother's house. They were distant cousins, very poor, and perhaps they never dreamed of leaving, because they died without ever even setting foot in the capital. They had planted, stirred, implored the earth. I saw them there under the sun, bent, toothless, incapable of coaxing forth life, in an unequal struggle with churlish nature not yet brought to heel even after more than two centuries. At six o'clock in the evening you could hear their breathing, like that of death, throughout the whole province, plunged into thick blackness. That was the time of tarantulas and fireflies and werewolves. My heart huddled in on itself.

I used to be afraid of the dark. I was afraid that the flame of the lamp would flicker so hard it would fall. The crickets accompanied the night with their long traumatizing songs.

But since then, the night has won me over to its cause of solitude, unobtrusive and infinite. I am overly reliant on its calm, making up for the years of unwarranted fear, of eyes shut tight. My only beautiful times have been in complete darkness and heavy rain. Every word of love, of fate, has taken the path of the night. Daytime is the cruel bearer of "I": it is all that light on the beaten earth of my childhood quarter, and on the marshes of Gros-Marin, and the Church of Saint Paul, and the runway of this airport—reality and its incomprehensible detours, its aches, its way of not making concessions.

My life went out like a wink, to be reignited in this mid-October. I was at the end of the trip and the beginning of silence. Or the other way around. The hours weighed heavily, especially the forgotten ones, lost in these trompe l'oeil paradises, this infinite jazz, rewound a hundred times. "How High Is the Moon?" "How Deep Is the Ocean?" Questions for forgetting, notes for leaving on overlong trips, for creating fragile, lying present tenses for oneself. It's death catching up with me now, an inexcusable folly.

XVI

The first city for those three women was Les Cayes, the main port city in the department of Sud, their first experience of the outside world. A caricature of a city plagued by hurricanes and floods. A city where four roads intersect that lead nowhere. I was a preteen when my mother took me there with so much pride. Her first city. She had lived there only a very short time. The normality was striking. My mother's family lived in what they called a city: two rows of houses facing each other across an unpaved street, built by the well-beloved president for life of the republic. I didn't belong in this place, either; I was in a black-and-white film, a walk-on, not even familiar with the plot.

The sewers seemed to call to us during the rare walks we took in the streets. Open sewers like mouths begging the sky for a few drops to make the mud that clogged their chests. Mouths with bad breath. Watchful mouths that did nothing to prevent the floods from washing away everything in the city. I thought of those walks four or five years later, sometime in a particular month of May, when the radio announced that the city of Les Cayes had been hit by a flood.

You never lingered on such trivial things. You couldn't go back and back forever over the lack of love and generosity. The city was bony and emaciated, like a woman who could no longer allow herself anything. Instead of colors, the pavement was covered with used clothing, old shoes from somewhere else being sold for cheap, which the poor leaped on, forcing some shops to close their doors. Her words accompanied by sweeping gestures, my mother tried to convince me of the former and current glories of the city I was seeing through a foreigner's eyes. It never opened itself up to me, that city. I navigated its ancient vetiver plantations, stole their scents, filled my head with them. That was it, the march of the seasons in this landlocked South that is almost unable to remember vetiver now, or the sea. I must have laughed back then, and learned, and mingled the vetiver and the sea with the odors of the sewers, because I could retrace my own steps years later. On the way to Grande'Anse I stopped in Les Cayes, and I found Maman's relative's house all by myself. She didn't recognize me, of course; she was sitting on her terrace, in her city, her hair white and wild. I should have reminded her who I was, reminded her of the time I spent with her a few years earlier. She offered me some bread. Held it out to me the way you hold out your hand. Once again, I didn't cry. I should have.

When I get back to the country, I'll wait a few days before I ask Maman if she's still alive. I can't ask her right away, can't add yet another story of death to the pile.

I wish I could go back toward that sea, toward the image of that old city aunt. She had children with sweet names, girls who remained virgins all their lives, I believe. People dismissed them as old maids, but there was nothing old about them in my child's eyes; they were full of feminine gentleness, a wholly provincial and very charming shyness. Among them were twin girls with light eyes, who moved apart a few years ago now, one living in Port-au-Prince and one still in Les Cayes. I promise myself I will stop and see how they are and also ask about the other people I am remembering right now, now that I know they are all gazing toward death, toward oblivion and solitude.

They all went there, the three sisters—Odile, Christie, and my mother—to that big city in Sud. They talked about it enthusiastically. My older brother, who was born there, always had an edge over me in their eyes, because I knew only the coarseness of Port-au-Prince. Les Cayes, to them, meant youth and the school, which none of them had attended for very long; it had been the first step toward somewhere else, the discovery of themselves and of how important it was to be beautiful when you are a woman. They had taken the vetiver-lined road together to Gelée—that's what the city's beach is called; it was once almost legendary for its beauty, before the general deterioration of everything in this country, especially the people. They had remembered the titles of the movies shown in the only theater in the city at the time, tried to pick up the thread of their lives like a forgotten piece of needlework, without ever managing to do it. All the legends had vanished; everything had become too big, too full.

In a few hours I will be back in that place where everyone jostles and shoves, as if engaged in an unending power struggle. I've planned it all out. From the painful stop at my mother's to the moment I slip back into my everyday silence. I have never told anything about my life, and so I will not tell anything this time. I wouldn't know how. I will give her the photo of her sister that I found, a photo in which she is beautiful and smiling, the way you should smile when you're alive and certain of being in the right place. I'll give her the booklet that was printed for the funeral, too, a pink booklet with another photo of her in which she's also very beautiful and all the names of the family members are full of typos, like some kind of bad joke. No one seems to have noticed. I am still a teacher at heart, even though since last year I haven't wanted to be a teacher anymore. I will be in a hurry to get back out into the street, and I will ask for my keys so I can get back quickly to the white walls of my apartment and my solitude, the only companions that await me, loyal and loving.

It'll be less painful at Maman's if it's a municipal water service day, one of the rare days when the tap is spitting the cloudy water that makes the whole quarter come running. It's like a dance. The dance of water, not very drinkable water. Drinking as if it's a task. Drops in which people could drown themselves. On the days when it happens, Maman is very busy filling up every vessel in the house that can be filled so she can give it away—or sell it to her neighbors, depending on her mood. She will never leave this quarter, Maman; she believes that she has had it all here, that she has it all. Water, and a telephone, and precious batteries to store electrical energy.

A green fruit in a large wastebasket. She loved that watercourse, Maman, loved for people to listen to her talk about the cretins at the distribution company who weren't doing their jobs. It got so that I would pretend to listen to Maman as she took refuge in household tasks when she was unhappy. When her niece died at eleven years old, she had washed every item of clothing in the house, a sort of catharsis. She'd spent hours kneeling at a washtub with a box of laundry soap, head bent so she wouldn't see anything, hear anything.

I want her to have water today; I could almost pray for it—I, who have never prayed. If God could make those cretins distribute the water today, she would be so much less unhappy; she would be distracted by the water, by the tap weeping in her stead, its cloudy water full of salt.

I haven't learned to live like my mother. She doesn't shut herself away. I might find her with three guests, her church companions, as it were. She's started going to church, undoubtedly figuring that, at a certain age, you have to turn back toward

God. She'll be in the midst of telling her friends, in the most romanticized way possible, about the strange foreign death of her sister, her life, her travels, which she considers to have been Christie's success. To have gone away, over there.

I sometimes had the impression that my mother was the axis around which the whole quarter revolved. Her actions impressed themselves deeply on it, morning and night. Maybe that's why I could never picture her anywhere else. The place had the dimensions of a country for her, a motherland. She knew everything that happened there, and once she began going to church with those other ladies, it got even worse. She said she was praying for me too. I needed it, she told me. I believed her. She sensed my drifting aimlessness, my solitude— but she had no words to speak to me about it, to console me. She was right, my mother: I was forever exceeding my quota of randomness and dissimilitude. Why else would I have drawn a curtain of silence over everything all those years? Why else would I have pitched my tent so far away, chosen to spend my time staring at ceilings, speaking a language the mad ones like me, the abnormal ones, called poetry?

Dina had drawn other horizons for herself elsewhere. That was her strength. She had swept it all away, erased it all. Even her memories. Especially her memories. She had wept like no one else at the Church of Saint Paul. Wept until she'd nearly fainted. Wept out of guilt, too, I know. I had wept with the same fervor and the same sincerity, once, out of guilt, for no real reason. I had wept over myself, for not having loved a man who left above all, but that is another story. I've been told she cried oceans of tears over her mother, too, and her little sister, and her father, with whom she hadn't spoken in more than fifteen years.

We don't speak the same language anymore. We've both forgotten the laughter of childhood. We look at each other politely without daring to speak, without finding space for the little iron bed we shared almost fifteen years ago, or the confidences whispered in the night. She had chosen real distance, distance of body, of language, of hopes. But that final death came to bore holes in her present, mixing it cruelly with her past. She inherited two little girls, she who had chosen not to have children.

I never thought of Dina. If she dies like the others in Florida, I will not make the journey. She won't make the journey if I die either. Two journeys saved, or two journeys lost. No coffee, no airport, no nostalgia.

I love the two little girls who have gone with Dina to her distant house in another city in the vastness of Florida, two little girls born in Florida but who will begin, only tomorrow, to understand foreignness in its full measure. The memory of those little girls is something pure and sweet. Will they remember the scent of incense? Perhaps those kilometers of asphalt will put some distance between them and their pain and that incense, like the smoke of childhood evaporating.

And so Dina will have failed, somewhere, to make a complete break, but she will continue to drape sheets over her memories, and I am sure she will drape them over those of the little girls, too, who have never seen the island, or the blue province, or the quarters filled with nameless people. I have always envied Dina her certainties. She went to public school, earned good grades that everyone talked about. She had interesting friends with bizarre names who told her love stories. She even went to church. She didn't need anyone; she didn't see anyone.

Sometimes when she walked, her feet didn't touch the ground. Now I realize that was because she didn't want to leave any footprints. She had planned it all perfectly, understood very early the way out.

Her mother and her aunt often reproached her, in the beginning, for not making friends from her own country; they didn't understand yet that her life began only once she'd arrived here. No more, no less. Maybe she had even lived their deaths. The words *nostalgia* and *regret* would baffle her, like when you hear words in a foreign language for the first time, a language so distant, so different from the one you speak that it makes you smile. Surely she had felt some guilt on that mid-October afternoon in the Church of Saint Paul. Was it Saint Paul? She must have asked herself, just once, and maybe for the only time, if she had been right—but she was doing well now. She had been right; she was sure of it. And in any case, it was too late.

XVII

I'm imagining, in this airport, mirrors in which travelers could look at themselves, the same way the whole quarter used to look at itself in the mirror that belonged to the neighbor across the street. That would make them less rushed. Less anxious.

Mirrors to fix in time the memory of their entire bodies, which, for a few hours, are about to defy the laws of weight and gravity enclosed in a plane. To look at their bodies like imprints on this blue space, in the best part of being alive. To live their dreams of beauty, their mortal dreams. Those travelers would see faces like mirages, just for the span of a look, a fleeting brilliance. I would seek, in the most complete randomness, those dreamed-of arms, honest and generous, that I have never known. This place would lose its banality then. For all those people who are, above all, startled by their differences, who don't look at one another, who mill and mingle without seeing each other, those mirrors would show their own image. Console them, perhaps, for their solitude. And that would make the time seem less long.

The mirrors would make it possible to save a few seconds of life from all the time lost; all those people hurrying past would believe themselves to be less sad. This airport would become like the quarter when our neighbor's mirror was there, filled with an artificial gaiety that would make them forget the terrorists, the loudspeakers and their threats, the fear of flying. Nothing but mirrors for seeing oneself, loving oneself! The world in this space is split between the desire to stay firmly anchored so as not to die and the urge to fly away and die three thousand feet in the air. The numbers of planes are dwindling, and the airlines are crying bankruptcy. *Where are the suicidal ones?* they seem to be asking.

The airport's glass walls offer generous blocks of sky into which I gaze, my eyes unfocused. I think of the paths of souls they told us about in the catechism classes of my childhood: those that lead to God, and those that lead to hell. I have never understood the meaning of sin, or God's instructions. I have spent very little time in churches, or pondering religion. My ideas about heaven and the sky have never grown up. So much the better. I never think about it. To live in harmony with the sky, and what goes on behind it, and those who live there—it's much better not to think about it.

It is beautiful, simply beautiful. Like that rainy October morning. Somewhere between that country and mine, the days stop mattering. The light on that day with its middling weather, a Tuesday or a Wednesday, painted the sorrowing faces light gray and pale yellow as they wept softly, elegantly. I had a rosary of first names, of half-lived moments, that created flawed, shaky memories—of nothing, of anything, of everything, of you all, and of you, who might be in New York or in Port-au-Prince, depending on whether my desires were seen from behind or head on.

No matter the day, or the place, I always sought a fool's solidarity and silence to finish a thirty-year-old story, a story that has done nothing but pulled down walls. In my city, the nights are stifling and hopeless. I had passed through them from one age to another in the reflection of full moons, in the shadow of stooping tendernesses. I had brought them back in my pocket: pebbles of solitude detached from the unknown. All my starting points were in pursuit of myself. I pleaded guilty to every charge held against me.

XVIII

There are so many signboards in this city, but there is nothing behind them. Everyone here, or nearly, has something to sell. Cheap trinkets and charms. They watch each other bursting with happiness amid the badly written, badly sung songs. Music doesn't know us, and we don't know how to make it. I've never loved any of our songs, and I wonder if Odile kept singing that sexist tune once she left our country, the one she sang that day at Maman's sewing machine. Songs are lightweight and durable possessions, after all.

One country cousin who smoked a pipe and swore like a sailor used to sing a lot when she came to the house. Her voice carried as far as the stink of her pipe. She embarrassed us, my brothers and me, and we wished we could hide her away, bury her, put her out like a candle so our classmates wouldn't see her or hear her, much less breathe in her smell. Her songs praised voodoo divinities and were peppered with dirty words that plunged us into a deep humiliation that's almost funny to think about now. We had other cousins who'd come to visit—they weren't real cousins, strictly speaking, but it was easier to think of them that way. The word *cousin* ended up being used to designate any irritating pain in the ass who came from the blue province or knew one of our parents. There were noisy ones, silent ones, mad ones, and they were all extremely poor. I might have remembered all those cousins if they'd known how to sing, but I remember only Odile's sexist song and the names of a few of the *loas* our cousin praised in her songs.

I wish I had a song from the old country, just a simple one. A song that belongs to everyone that I could sing in this airport, a song that would surprise these travelers, and maybe make them smile. The way people tend to smile at craziness. Where I come from, madness makes people laugh. It's amusing. My people elect maniacs to public office. Maniacs who amuse, and destroy, and enjoy playing absolutely irresistible adult games. Every quarter has its madman or madwoman, and if there isn't one, the people create them. Mad people who smash the city's many signs. Painted signs, and neon ones that rarely light up. The signs predate the shops, and the schools, and the churches, and the *banques de borlette*, and they survive them. Being seen is important.

My father told us that our family used to be rich and famous. Generals who had waged war; industrialists who had fed the whole region of Nord with cassava. He needed that glorious past, and a glorious present, too, to live. Every week he'd say he was about to start writing his book. I don't think he knows what it's going to be about even now. Maman always said he was nothing but a liar. That word hurts me now. I think he's a dreamer who never saw his famous-general ancestors come back from the war. He's still looking for that someone else that he isn't and that he is. In his quiet moments, he must see them comparing him to themselves and hating him.

I never ask him questions; he'd only get angry anyway. He and Maman are always together, but they hardly speak, or just argue drearily. Nothing has ever been done right, according to them. I imagine I'm probably one of those incorrectly done things, with my drifting, and my escapes, and my shameless, disjointed writing.

Nothing can be redone on these paths to death. We're all doomed. All we do is watch the spectacle unfold, pretending not to see anything. Bad actresses, bad casting. The dream of exile has evaporated, and the ones who did manage it died of it. It's a closed book now: a story that makes you gaze into the void, and back up sometimes, but all alone, truly, completely alone, the way I am now.

My stories have always come to me when they're already in progress, almost over, even my love stories. I have hidden myself too often beneath words and their images; I've only ever just brushed the surface of anything, I am nothing but a memory trying to exist, and no one would notice, possibly, if I disappeared. I tell myself that no one sees me in this airport;

my fate is to be a fleeting memory. I would like to learn the business of everyday life, real life, quivering and ever changing.

I am dying. They say that dying people see their lives flash past before their eyes, all the images they've pretended to forget, the words said, and badly said, and missed. I've taken the shortcut of nights to find myself here, alone, with my bleeding cities and my catch-up lives. I have nothing now but poorly loved once upon a times, cords floating above me that I cannot grasp.

A lineup of banal things, ordinary people jerked awake by death, death past and present, and guilt for sorrows missed and the wrath of that city forever undiscovered.

XIX

It was a June afternoon, the dust so thick it was almost impossible to see what was happening around you. I walked the dirty sidewalks of Port-au-Prince with words that wanted to tell, to put down roots for me, a history. The afternoon light was fading, and no one spoke, or at least I didn't hear anyone, and the same desire gripped me, the desire not to go home. Maman saw a tendency toward vagabondage in that desire, and it grieved her.

A dry, futureless afternoon that could sum up my life. I walked toward that school where I was learning noise and all sorts of useless things. A June afternoon on which I was taking my torments out for a stroll. I was covered with a veil of dust. Everything had always been linear, ageless, without a single dream to keep warm for tomorrow, like here, now. And from all of that I created my own exile, an exile leading even further away, an exile that made me blind and mute.

That wandering multitude could see nothing, hear nothing; it was nothing but an extension of the tentacles of that city where the streets are pathways to suicide. It seems that I was born there, in the month of June, of course. We have never loved each other, this city and me.

My memory is strolling now through its criminal nights, a catastrophic confession of an identity found despite myself, always through the door of words and in the unfinished movement of a little girl dancing in an already old photograph. Colors and perfumes have mingled too often on these sidewalks. Sun, blood, filth, corpses, public spectacles, firsts in a pretend city without benches, without gardens, where you hear in an infinite echo the voice of the open sewers.

Everything is for sale here. Especially these broken, wasted faces trotted out on small screens the world over, in newspapers whose stock-in-trade is pity. Pity is humanitarian aid, too, and compassion. Every story ends in scenes of war. The banal stories and the stupid ones, the stories about very little and the stories about nothing. I'm one of those who goes along their way without looking, because, quite simply, I'm afraid. I know the image is harder to wash away than the bloodstain.

I hear half-murmured calls for help in the moonless nights when not even a dog barks. Living is unstylish in the wee hours, stiff and rigid. And yet the nights are short, those nights when I stand guard at wordpoint, perched on songs that would like to be cries of love thrown in the faces of the latest breezes carrying bad news.

It was a June day, and the city was jammed, shanty on top of shanty, despair upon despair, with the breath of elsewhere. I was there in that endless break, that set-in-stone June afternoon. That space between day and night. Twenty-eight thousand square kilometers of bends and detours and U-turns. Of graffiti to scratch into stones to write a story the way you beg forgiveness, a story to throw into the sea as a symbol of togetherness with those souls, those bodies that fled to end their days in Floridian cemeteries.

A passenger as much as one can be, muffled up in my heritage of shadow and silence. It is October; it could have been June, or another month. The months, the hours, the days are simply metaphors for that great wound in the shape of an island, a great scar splitting the Caribbean Sea, starkly frank in its misery. I was a passenger in this gallery of suspicious people, of potential terrorists. It's a time of war and horror, a war like none that has ever been waged before, so blind and unilateral is it.

I stagger from minute to minute, from word to word, as my city draws near in a cloudy story, cloudy like those days after the rains, those days when the whole city was driven toward the sea, men and women and children and houses. Peals and peals of laughter, silenced in the blink of an eye. Seconds given back to the void. Spaces surrendered to the water, and the winds, and the silt.

My arms are outstretched in these overlong sleeves. Triviality comforts, fortunately. A bookmark on a blank page to mark the absence of a story, words, fatigue.

The toothless quarters breathed softly, shallowly, the way dying people often do. The gutted walls told us only things we already knew. You hurtled quickly into forgetfulness until the next flood, the next war. The sad image passing was that of my mother going to pray. Her Bible, her hymnbook, her defeats, her solitudes had become her shadow. I had always detested my image in the mirror, in which I looked like one or the other of my parents. I knew that was because I was afraid of taking it all on, that terrible feeling of heaviness that clung to things without anyone even trying to find out where the truth lay.

She walked in the afternoon, her shadow taking up more room than she did; she seemed to want to elbow it aside at certain moments. I wondered what she was thinking. She clutched her Bible in her arms, and her hymnbook, and her afternoon. She had stopped time in her own life, this oldest of the sisters from the blue province. She didn't know yet, on that day, that she would outlive the other two, and I loved her in her detachment, her resistance, despite herself, to the onslaughts of the quarter, and the city, and time.

It must be true that God remains the sole recourse of the despairing. People pray a lot in my country, and the more they pray, the deeper they sink. And I sink with them—I, who never pray. We all live in the flickering of a pale flame that lights only paths of blood and misfortune, and it was these paths that Christie, Odile, Dina, Rachel had traveled to America, the America of wars and dreams of glory and of fortune.

And so she went on her fragile way, my mother. Never took risks. Almost never had opinions. She had taken on the truths of those close to her the way you marry a husband chosen by your family. Happiness was tranquility, the certainty that today and tomorrow would be the same.

In a few days it will be November. The Day of the Dead, when bodies are disinterred. Fear of speaking will bring together our escape routes, begin another age of emptiness and tendernesses not given; on either side of our gazes, the pain will meet. We will imagine letters never written, wrongs never imputed. We will all be equal: we don't know how to grieve; we don't take care of our dead; we live with them like shameful maladies; we hide them, protect them without ever being able to speak of them, like frostbite of the soul.

November will not look like June, uncertainties and dreams bivouacking together in the capital. November is the heavy weight of short days, the urge for oblivion, the hope of the mythical days of childhood, cigarettes lit in the depths of the night to create convictions, for prisons to leap over quotation marks and dissolve in the withered city, disjointed, fragmented like the brief poetry on the page that slumbers beneath my fingers. There will be no open arms, no outstretched hands. This will be nothing new. We will have to move forward in the barrenness and coagulation of our memories. Identity will be like an image of religion or politics, causing whole crowds to surge with the stains on their tongues and shoulders of false kisses and blasphemy.

The capital of slag and cinders, of discarded seas, will offer me again its generosity, its storms and floods recurring over and over like orgasms. My solitude will remain unthreatened. My family and I will forgo the sham of the Day of the Dead, of a pious November, and continue to flaunt our wounds. Blinded windows overlooking the cemetery of America.

My premature exhaustion, my one-way trips, will elicit no comment; our silences will be acceptable, even willingly shared. We needed only chance to go faster, short toll roads to lose our similarities, to propose other stories without this warped quarter, without a radio, without a mirror. The illusion will seem real for as long as the Day of the Dead lasts.

XX

The story gets away from me occasionally. I search the faces of the passing pilots for that tourist-friendly smile I used to see before the terrorists attacked. The pilots have done a good job of hiding their anguish beneath their pale skin. They exchange looks of extreme unction; their mouths have already known last kisses. Myself, I'm looking for one that will be the first, just to get a grip on the story, to give it some appearance of beginning. Every detail here is different from my everyday spaces, but I have the same feeling of places with no exit, that tomorrow will never come.

Necklaces of words and looks that bestow neither beauty nor difference. People look at one another without seeing each other; it's a mania, a North American quality. Discretion and indifference are the same words, you might say. I could be wrong. Doesn't matter. I'm here only for a few coffees and to wait for a plane that will take me home to that place of mad things, to my island that dances, eyes closed, that has retained, for me, the fresh scent of the air after rain and a great gulp of chaos to welcome me back to solitude.

My piecemeal story, almost without a beginning, wouldn't be worthy of four lines in these full-color major newspapers. The third world will send plenty of others off to die, and the cemeteries will still be full. The only particularity of this story is that it could never be more than four lines, doesn't even need a photo, even in the worst Florida-backwater rag, for one to know the itinerary of that voyage, to spot the metaphors for death.

I've broken out of my prisons without a commotion, without a riot. Love is a footnote everywhere on my list of truths. I've long believed in changes in the weather, in the evidence of us, of our existence. A dozen first names that don't even give a real and lasting image. I'm like the old grandfather clock in Maman's living room: I have no memory. I go around in circles like that clock in this airport—every hour, every minute, every second foreign, pointless, futureless.

It keeps ticking even now, moving forward like a blind person in time. That clock and Linda the sewing machine are living objects; they are part of our history, like little sisters with Down syndrome who have always been kept at home, and whom everyone knows will never leave. The clock must be counting down, even now, the time left until my return to the country and how long it will take me to come to the house. It was patient like Maman, that clock. Certain, like she was, that it could change nothing in the course of our lives, or in the destiny of this country with its furious tempo like a machine operated by madmen. It existed, like her, in time irreconcilable with life.

Each morning is the start of a new war against nature, against misery, against oneself or one's neighbor. Survival has many meanings and almost no purpose. I had sought my dream, my elsewhere, in the memory of the old burned-out streetlamps of my city, wondering whom I had truly loved, what I had kept as a loving memory in this tangled mess. My city that goes to bed early, without taxis, without illusions, with no great mystery, my blind city. From here I can't hear the obsessive music of its misery that makes children dance in the street.

If I had someone to talk to right now in this airport, I would speak fast, still trying to hide myself, to cast a fog over everything, to blur the traces of the looming sea and of lost memory, and my many coffees, and my fear, and my yearning to go back. I murmur first names without any certainty, first names hung on my Port-au-Prince days like lies, first names that often have smiling faces, faces that prolong my search, whirling around the words and around a drink, faces to make me forget that death might be lying in wait around the very next corner, an amiable and assured death that we have learned to look right in the eye.

I can see them already, those faces, hear them, those every-day voices, each playing their role with care. Our plans have always been fragmentary, like the ones for great love unveiled on Friday nights that have given us scraps of memories, louder notes in the monotone whole, in the weary gleam of our cigarettes. You died again and again in echoes of voices, in those songs learned by heart like toys of sorrowing childhood. I will continue to live these signaled ends, these solitudes disguised, some nights, by bursts of laughter. Laughter like Christie's in the photo, laughter meant to conceal misery, conceal pain, conceal worry.

And yet our gazes never want to kill themselves. They continue to follow the torturous paths of life, if only we really believed them. Our pockets are filled with exile that we take out to console ourselves for our own unhappiness. No one is wrong. Ever.

XXI

October lingers here with its changing moods, the aftertaste of its great defeats. The America that knew so well how to create legions of walking wounded for itself—America, the righter of wrongs and giver of lessons—had been attacked and had responded. They didn't think here; they acted. I burrowed deeper into my individuality; I was even more lost, more alone. It was necessary to fly away, for everything to fly away.

Despairingly, my eyes scan these blank walls, these chairs, these shops, these people with long paths and immense horizons, and I can no longer feel my being—my story made of circles, falls, and breaks. I must gather it all up, down to the last crumb. It is a story that will only grow in my homeland.

It's time to go back. The voice in the loudspeaker isn't the one I want to hear: it doesn't console me, doesn't soothe me. The line of passengers forms quickly. Going back is pleasant, I imagine, for most of these travelers, each with their own share of war, their own share of death.

THE DAYS THAT FOLLOW

My dream has remained suspended somewhere in this backyard. No matter how many times I change my clothes or my vocabulary, this life of mine continues to show through, and this quarter, these now formless faces that rub shoulders with death more often than life, like all those people on the sidewalks. The city has been waiting for me, like a faithful lover with whom I am happily reuniting—the first day in the same ideas, the same misery. The cries and the silences serve as my entourage.

Today is Tuesday. I was born on a Tuesday; it means nothing. I know this road well, a road that led me so far away from words of love, so far from dreams, a road worn smooth. The driver doesn't speak. I'm grateful to him for that. October is spreading out its bright sun like a carpet; I'm already saturated with the noises of the street. Windows rolled down, I take my place amid the buzz. I was only in that other hell for four days, hemmed in by regulations and silences and deliberate games, and everywhere the odor of terrorism, the arrogance of people who are right even before the question is posed. And death.

A line of little girls dressed in pink files along the sidewalk: it's a school day, a normal day casting its circle of sunlight on the little heads. The city will soon buckle under its own weight; everyone knows it. It is overflowing with everything. With me, especially, today. I am like a piece of bad news. On the walls I spot a few tattered posters from the last elections, nothing but portraits of men with false smiles, nothing to do with Christie's laughter in the green leafiness of the blue province that I'm afraid I will never see again, with my dearth of courage, and my emptied-out dreams, and my lack of energy. I have never lived anywhere else, but I can't feel my roots here.

It doesn't take long to cross the city, the quarters blurring together. The time passes faster than the street images, the noises. I have to get out of the car and walk; I have always entered this quarter on foot, walking on the sand and the rocks. This quarter is forever building itself, day and night: stroke of water, stroke of shadow, then retreat. The ugliness is surely irreversible. As always, I can feel eyes on me; I don't see anyone, but I know they are watching from behind windows and doors. I could walk with my eyes closed, so well do I know my way around here, if not for the risk of falling in the sand. I would have loved to walk with my eyes closed; I hate it so much.

I push open the gate. I am back. Maman is there. She looks at me. Her eyes are always strange, something like a tinge of blue around her pupils but which is not blue. I was wrong; there's nothing she's expecting me to say, and I say nothing. Why, after all, should we break the silence? There is nothing to tell. Not right away. She chooses to slice into the silence with a coffee.

The coffee has been made for years now in an Italian cafetière. Still the same one, shaped like an hourglass. The little appliance has always fascinated me. The ritual of the coffee, our mutual history with the beverage soothes me. My mother's movements are still the same as always. She is like the earth, rotating on her axis, imperturbable. We're in a silent film; we've spent our lives learning our roles. We are perfect.

After all, why should we, even once, break this silence that has become one of the only things we have in common? My mother turns on her axis as she has always done, with natural movements that, it seems, nothing can stop: not my eyes fixed on her as if for the first time, nor the ceaseless racket of passersby with buckets that are invariably empty, eternal conquistadors in search of the water so rare in the poor quarters. There is no radio to fill the silence, not our own devastating news nor that of others. I look at my suitcase on the floor. I am as foreign here as I was at the Miami airport. I have to be going, I say. It's getting late. It's a Tuesday in late October.

Wednesday and one more day. Objects scattered on the floor uncertainly, wholly southern anxiety, like a silent sea, terrified of being, some days, the mirror of this city. I surge and retreat like a wave, rebellious and resigned to unhappiness. The white door of my bedroom is reflected in the mirror; I have no hope of anything. The child I made one April day is still asleep, serene in her four years, her life hardly different from that of the stuffed bear sleeping by her side. Every move she makes overlaps with my life, my dreams. My child, my act of failed love for whom, some days, I curate another memory, outside the commotion in my head, in the chance and the certainty of songs found, almost as I have found, in a stroke of madness, a warm breeze.

Wednesday knocks at my door in city clothes. I must forget; I must continue to live. I join the game. Everything appears easy; everything is scheduled. I am a laborer of the useful. I am a woman. In a few minutes I will be behind a desk with a ringing telephone. I will take up my place in a conventional setting. I will find a useless identity, trivial, overrated. I will go back, willing and anonymous, to that airport. I wish I could watch myself pass, start the parade of my ghosts and my regrets all over again. Wednesday to shake off the ashes and the grief, to see myself in color again, to open my eyes to its chaos, the bright light of Wednesday, heavy and impatient to end its race. Dust accumulates on the actions of the passersby. I am afraid, and I replicate dangerously my movements of the previous night. The same complaint echoes infinitely in my head, and my gaze explodes into a thousand shards. From my mirror to the street I am in transit, without an identity. Misery stretches in slow shadows from both sides of my new quarter for all that is happy behind its high walls, behind which I have been living in a kind of tormented exile for two years, as if you can hide from your own troubles, your own living past. Wednesday glides smoothly over my skin. I am fully integrated into the indifferent flow of these hemmed-in days in this phantom country.

I know of no way of living, no song able to evade the grip of daily life here. I turn on the radio, which reminds me that there are assassins in the city, sadly arrogant and lawful. From daybreak to the last spark of sunset, the colors rebel, a merciless battle to separate from one another, to defeat what remains of life here. To burst the abscess. Wednesday amid all the sorrows, amid the other days, wordless and comfortless, mine in all this space, in all my emptiness.

Thursday rises in white smoke on the mountain. I can hardly live in my own body. My thoughts whirl round and round; I have kept clenched in my hands the image of a cemetery somewhere deep in Florida. I open and close them, ten fingers and a heart in a conversation of despair. My fragile present falters, stiffens, rights itself; I am a space between two scenes, a gasp of breath.

The house is small, the walls seeming as if they want to close in on each other some days; everything is white, and I allow myself to play with the furniture, the false docility of the doors. I struck up a slow conversation with the ceiling the other day. It's white like the seven nights of my week, like that path on which my story is walking backward, my story shared years in advance, lives in advance.

There isn't much distance between the pieces of furniture, a blurring between the necessary and the incidental. It's a familiar Thursday morning that begins with a coffee, my greatest inheritance, my slow path ahead of myself at the airport in Florida, and from the airport in Florida to this narrow house that helps me to hide my lies, to hide myself, and to play, some days, the game of happiness and love.

There is a wound in the white tablecloth, a big hole that should lead toward the sea, toward the dreamed-of unknown of silence. I dip a finger in, and I taste. I am publicly alive, with a passport and an ID, and I measure my steps on this surface that holds out a hand to the smoke, to bodies pierced, emptied, ill at ease.

Thursday shoves me into a landscape of shadow. I turn around and around in a forest of familiar sounds, tortured pages, unable to reach the end of my cry, unable to cross this space.

The house closes in on me more and more; I am sitting around this table of companions, endlessly rooting in the wound, standing guard over my dead. Rain pounds on the door and the window. I jump. I don't open them. It is confident, it is timid, and I offer my orphaned gaze to the purity of the drops caught up in the endurance of the game, a slow drumming on the windows, like my recent past. Life goes on its way into my head like a familiar, nagging song. Thursday takes me away like a lullaby. I will close my eyes to undo my bonds to this white space, this placeless space that drives out my memory. This day has taught me nothing.

The armoire opens like an eye watching me. I look at the neat row of clothes, clothes that have not forgotten my mad desire to be someone else. I drop my gaze, filled with a kind of shame.

X

Friday shatters the morning sun. Yesterday's rain persists gently. I linger in front of my mirror, exhaling great clouds from a cold cigarette. I am a sort of stain in this house; the mirror captures me entirely. I don't like myself.

I'm standing in front of these clothes, all suffused with my perfume. Too much of me. I have always kept too much space for myself. I overwhelm myself. I'm suffocating in all this space. I hide behind my yellowed pages. The books were the only things that came with me when I moved out of my former lives. I have spoken about Marcel Proust far more than I have about my own people. I am ashamed.

The morning set in early. No sun. My desire to be loved, which I have falsified over these past few days, has resumed its place, heavier than my thirty years of secrets. It's seven fifteen in the morning, and the sun continues to turn its back on the city, which is already quaking at the threat of continued rain. The living and the dead are afraid. I sit on the edge of the bed, and my games smash in the mirror into inaudible shards that stumble slowly around the room.

I leave the house like a cold wind, descending into the sluggish monotony of Pétion-Ville, that deceitful city that is so good at hiding its shantytowns behind dollarized shops without elegance. I am steeping, as I do each morning, in its chronic coldness, its roads that don't lead very far, and the distance it allows itself to give. I prefer the night, with its mournful whores offering themselves body and voice to customers who would never set about writing a memoir. Oblivion is a future profession I ought, perhaps, to learn.

For a long time I have been intrigued by this city, so far and so different from my quarter. I wanted to exchange habits with it, to enter into it the way you join a new family in another country. Today, it is merging with the tottering whole that threatens to crush everything below; I always suffer it like a blast of wind, hot or cold, and in it I remain wholly foreign.

Friday gauges itself against the lethargy of this city, timid and with no great attraction; an old troubadour exhausts himself in his song. People are afraid to dream, and yet it is a familiar refrain, a famous one. I tell myself that they must be humming in their heads anyway. You never know.

The night is a bandage hiding a thousand wounds and a thousand words, and I rest my head on a secondhand shoulder in this noisy bar where I come to listen to the same songs every Friday night.

I'm once again facing the mirror in the ladies' room of this bar where I have sometimes burst into laughter. I have circles beneath my eyes and red lips; Friday-night makeup is thick and deceptive, makeup to create a woman who is good at dancing, good at pretending. I enjoy the calm of this stinking bathroom; I feel like going to sleep.

)(

A spot on the white floor and the hell of clattering pots, the grease splattering my will to live. Saturday, undone like a hairdo, relentlessly resumes its banal household refrain. The coffee cups float in the foam-filled sink, clouds of memory, fragile bubbles floating on the eternity of sorrows. I dip my hand fearfully into the cold water and drown the drops of coffee, drown the orange-tinted morning that is trying to slip in through the window.

Saturday, blended with traces of sleep, remembers nothing; it makes a sun to order for itself, like a self-conscious smile. I close behind me the door of this house erased by its own discretion that keeps hold of great treasures of silence and the echo of my empty laughter. Since I changed my starting point and my routine, I take only paths that run in straight lines, hopping as best I can over the puddles of memory left by my old floods.

I have created suits and ceremonies for myself, words and smiles that sparkle, real-false jewels in the decor of the streets through which I walk, soul dormant, eyes tinted, abandoning myself to the stoic game of wanting to live, of pretending.

Saturday becomes, in my head, a great carousel whirling around stains and faded ink, an enormous blur in which a few dreams and necessities accumulate. I request an advance on memories not yet experienced: the breath of a lover who will stay only a little while, requiring nothing, no letter to keep, no picture together with bright-white smiles, no hope of posterity.

Saturday is a damp cigarette stub that I put between my lips with disgust, that I put between my lips anyway, the same way I set foot on the too-clean floor at five o'clock in the morning to run toward my death indissociable from the getting by, the daily life, and I frown at my regular life that fills boxes of forms at the consulate and in unknown archives.

The day breaks and is lost in the furor of the supermarkets; I stop and let baskets and bags pass. The city's heart is bent like a diseased tree. The smiles have blind spots. I hold out my hand to catch a few drops of late October falling like tears on the faces of pedestrians who run so as not to get wet. October, Saturday becomes a deserted pavement and crevices that fill with dirty water. October, Saturday is a time like another that passes; it is a day after the days that age me and swing me toward oblivion.

I don't want to mourn anyone. The television sends back a thousand colors that mingle with the white of my bedroom. It's ten o'clock and a few minutes of convinced silence and solitary seconds, without a spot on the parquet floor, without a plan. The night has wound back its watch. At this precise moment, I should have looked for God's part in my story.

Leaving day gulps down its brew of regret, fatal illness, and false hope; life relentlessly continues its course with its tang of the sea and its boundless and falsely friendly calm. My fingers grope along the sheets for the remains of companionship left by those bodies before today, without importance, without future. My Sundayed desires have a vague memory of finished stories, open eyes on a random dawn in a northern country with public space beneath the windows and hotels for tourists with credit cards and a tendency toward obesity.

I would like many seventh days with public space beneath my windows, prostitutes like boils on the story, to rewrite the city church by church, to cover myself with white tablecloths and lose myself in their labyrinthine embroidery.

I am a witness to the slow death of my land, to its inexorable slide toward a foreign elsewhere, toward the sea, toward abysses near and far. My loss is imminent; no Sunday has relit my flame despite a thousand sleeps, a thousand prayers. I remain unforgivably confused. I never know if this is the last or the first day of the week. My mother knows. She must have taken the path to church this morning, trusting, willing, bolstered by her ways of the cross and her prayers. I envy her her certainties; I have been chronically without any for thirty years and dozens of Sundays.

Sunday, warm voices and life mingle with bread crumbs. I pry into the left-hand part of the day. I tremble. I spew words without rereading them. The lines stretch out, slow ropes hanging over the cemeteries and all the brown clinging to my temples and my falsely adorned heart, my heart that dries out the blood.

Sunday is an immense church swollen with the vanity of living and of being beautiful. I lean against the wall, and the room rotates on itself, on me. The weather is bad in my eyes, and my body pales; Sunday is white like my room. Sunday has no reflection in my mirror and sweats out a song that I know, a song that makes me afraid.

The golden pelt of the day stretches as far as the eye can see. The city is still sleepy, caught between the fires of misery and steps that are too heavy, words that echo too loudly.

Blue

𝕏

It's the end of a story; it's a normal Monday in which nothing soothes. The street is a reproduction of our gaping wounds. Monday is a bad day to dream of a life without title, without social or marital status, without obligation. The pavement is crowded with old things. I take shape in reality, I am alive, and I open my eyes to the colors and the movements. I create a first day for myself, telling myself that I have the right to it.

I hold a handful of the sea, gentle and blue like the province that is sinking deeper and deeper into my memory; I am still late for one or two pointless battles, lost in advance. Monday of making do paves the streets, turns the knobs of my doors, and wakes me up from my deaths. Florida, as vast as the desires of the men and women here, hides behind measured gestures and friendly smiles. Time passes inexorably and trivially; my story will be neither told nor written. It is in the ordinary playing out of a common Monday, and it yields up its place.

The radio mirrors my voice, my resemblance to you all; it is an oddly present afterlife echo. I repeat the same things for hours until I am exhausted, stirring up again and again the fatigue and the desolation. I turn my wound into a brooch that I pin on Monday, a Sunday outfit, an everyday outfit.

The difficult morning awakening follows me at every step, more alive than my ghosts. I appreciate the certainty of my

115

civil-servant fatigue and the cowardice that pricks me like a needle. I pay dearly the price of being alive and not free, far from the old quarter where the stones grow faster than the children. Seasons germinate in my head, old paths, cities where solitude is legal, where I put white ribbons on the landscape like there were at the Easter communion I took once and that I don't remember anymore.

I spell out your bodies letter by letter so as not to forget them, Monday's necessity hammering violently at my mind. I am blinded by hollowness, and I weep. I am holding on to these memories with one hand, and I lean to one side. Your bodies unravel one by one, and so the only soil that belongs to us will be the soil on our bodies, here or elsewhere, at the whim of exile and misery.

All of this is without fulfillment, without reason. You've realized that, fortunately. There is no body anymore, no songs, no quarters of stones and mirrors. This fable has merely lived too long, dragged along too many lost words, too many rebellious words. Monday mingles with the other days until it resembles a final day, a day that makes allowances, that goes so far as to blend with the night, and all the nights, and all the other days. A day with dreams of white tablecloths and fortune.

Monday goes on its way, without glory. It wasn't foreseen that we would leave, not agreed upon that we would love, that what seemed to have been given to us would be taken back, like a fickle heart. And I am alone with a story that ends without a splash, unseen.

ABOUT THE AUTHOR

Photo © Homère Cardichon

Born in Port-au-Prince, where she still resides, Emmelie Prophète is a poet, novelist, journalist, and director of the National Library of Haiti. Her publications include *Blue (Le testament des solitudes)*, which earned her the Grand Prix littéraire de l'Association des écrivains de langue française (ADELF) in 2009; *Le reste du temps* (2010), which tells the story of her special relationship with journalist Jean Dominique, who was murdered in 2000; *Impasse Dignité* (2012); and *Le bout du monde est une fenêtre* (2015).

ABOUT THE TRANSLATOR

Translator Tina Kover is an American-born literary translator specializing in both classic and modern literature, including Négar Djavadi's *Disoriental*, Alexandre Dumas's *Georges*, and Mahir Guven's Goncourt Prize–winning *Older Brother*. Her work has won the Albertine Prize and the Lambda Literary Award in Bisexual Fiction and has been shortlisted for the International Dublin Literary Award, the National Book Award for Translated

Literature, the PEN Translation Prize, the Warwick Prize for Women in Translation, the Oxford-Weidenfeld Translation Prize, and the Scott Moncrieff Prize. She is also cofounder of the YouTube channel Translators Aloud, which spotlights readings by literary translators from their own work.